"There's no need to apologize."

Amusement danced in his gaze. "I wasn't planning to. As far as I know, it isn't a crime to kiss royalty in Carramer, especially when it's by invitation."

"You're imagining things."

"Guilty as charged," he agreed, without the slightest trace of remorse. "I wasn't the only one. Your imagination was working overtime, as well, my beautiful princess."

Her anger flared, a close cousin to frustration. In his arms she *had* imagined all sorts of possibilities, most revolving around the drifts of sweet-smelling hay around their feet, inviting them to sink down and take the exploration so much further. Knowing it was impossible left her aching with disappointment.

She was appalled at herself. How could she feel this way about someone she had good reason to dislike? His willingness to use what he knew about her to get what he wanted was bad enough. So why did she yearn so for his touch?

Dear Reader,

Silhouette's 20th anniversary celebration continues this month in Romance, with more not-to-be-missed novels that take you on the romantic journey from courtship to commitment.

First we revisit STORKVILLE, USA, where a jaded Native American rancher seems interested in *His Expectant Neighbor*. Don't miss this second book in the series by Susan Meier! Next, *New York Times* bestselling author Kasey Michaels returns to the lineup, launching her new miniseries, THE CHANDLERS REQUEST.... One bride, *two* grooms—who will end up *Marrying Maddy*? In *Daddy in Dress Blues* by Cathie Linz, a Marine embarks on his most terrifying mission—fatherhood!—with the help of a pretty preschool teacher.

Then Valerie Parv whisks us to a faraway kingdom as THE CARRAMER CROWN continues. *The Princess's Proposal* puts the lovely Adrienne and her American nemesis on a collision course with...love. The ever-delightful Terry Essig tells the tale of a bachelor, his orphaned brood and the woman who sparks *A Gleam in His Eye*. Shhh.... We can't give anything away, but you *must* learn *The Librarian's Secret Wish*. Carol Grace knows...and she's anxious to tell you!

Next month, look for another installment of STORKVILLE, USA, and THE CHANDLERS REQUEST...from *New York Times* bestselling author Kasey Michaels. Plus, Donna Clayton launches her newest miniseries, SINGLE DOCTOR DADS!

Happy Reading!

Mary-Theresa Hussey

Mary-Theresa Hussey
Senior Editor

Please address questions and book requests to:
Silhouette Reader Service
U.S.: 3010 Walden Ave., P.O. Box 1325, Buffalo, NY 14269
Canadian: P.O. Box 609, Fort Erie, Ont. L2A 5X3

The Princess's Proposal

VALERIE PARV

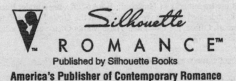

ROMANCE™

Published by Silhouette Books

America's Publisher of Contemporary Romance

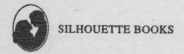

SILHOUETTE BOOKS

ISBN 0-373-19471-4

THE PRINCESS'S PROPOSAL

Copyright © 2000 by Valerie Parv

This edition published by arrangement with Harlequin Books S.A.

Visit Silhouette at www.eHarlequin.com

Printed in U.S.A.

Books by Valerie Parv

Silhouette Romance

The Leopard Tree #507
The Billionaire's Baby Chase #1270
Baby Wishes and Bachelor Kisses #1313
*The Monarch's Son #1459
*The Prince's Bride-To-Be #1465
*The Princess's Proposal #1471

*The Carramer Crown

VALERIE PARV

lives and breathes romance and has even written a guide to being romantic, crediting her cartoonist husband of nearly thirty years as her inspiration. As a former buffalo and crocodile hunter in Australia's Northern Territory, he's ready-made hero material, she says.

When not writing her novels and nonfiction books, or speaking about romance on Australian radio and television, Valerie enjoys dollhouses, being a *Star Trek* fan and playing with food (in cooking, that is). Valerie agrees with actor Nichelle Nichols, who said, "The difference between fantasy and fact is that fantasy simply hasn't happened yet."

HISTORY OF CARRAMER

The Carramer Crown takes place in the fictitious island kingdom of Carramer in the South Pacific. French explorer la Perouse called Carramer "the loveliest fleet of islands anchored in any ocean." Carramer comprises three inhabited islands and a handful of tiny offshore islands. The main island is Celeste, home to the capital city of Solano, and the ruling monarch, Lorne de Marigny. Across the Carramer Strait lies the larger, blissfully beautiful Isle des Anges (Island of the Angels) and its near neighbor, tiny Nuee, both governed by Prince Lorne's younger brother, Michel, next in line to the throne after Lorne's son, Nori. Younger sister Adrienne sees no role for herself in government and yearns to establish a horse-breeding stable.

Carramer's traditions are a mixture of French and Polynesian influences. It enjoys a perfect climate, as near-constant trade winds prevail throughout the year, and most rain falls as daytime showers that are accompanied by rainbows, giving rise to the popular name for Carramer of "the Rainbow Isles."

There is rumored to be another royal offspring living in the United States, but so far that story remains untold.

Valerie Parv
Official historian to the sovereign state of Carramer

Chapter One

"Would you like a balloon, miss? Souvenir of the Nuee Fair."

Adrienne tensed involuntarily as the fairground hawker approached her, then told herself that he couldn't possibly know who she was, far less that he was trying to sell one of his metallic silver creations to Her Highness, Princess Adrienne de Marigny, daughter of the ruling house of Carramer.

Her simply cut navy pants and white hand-knit shell had been chosen to ensure that she blended in with the thousands of people attending Nuee's annual Fair and Horse Show. Her straw sunhat and dark glasses not only disguised her much-photographed features and waterfall of glossy raven hair, they protected her delicate skin from the hot afternoon sun, as well.

A sense of adventure caught hold of her and she smiled at the hawker. The last time she was offered a balloon, she had been eight years old and a nanny had purchased and carried it for her. Adrienne had attended other fairs since then, but always in an official role. Today there was no one to tell her how unseemly it was for a princess to carry such a frivolous toy. "I'd love one, thank you."

The hawker grinned back. "Choose any one you like. Of course, a pretty girl like you should let the man in your life buy it for you."

"He might if there was one," she said. The man probably called every woman under a hundred a pretty girl, unaware that, as a princess, Adrienne was as restricted in her choice of men as she was in where she went and what she did.

If her brothers, Lorne and Michel, knew she was out in disguise and unescorted, they'd have a fit, especially her older brother Lorne, she thought, picturing his frown of disapproval. Their parents had died when she was much younger, so Lorne considered himself her guardian as well as her monarch. She knew her brother only wanted what was best for her, but she felt that at twenty-three years old she was capable of taking care of herself.

With both her brothers safely married now, her role as royal hostess was much reduced, too. At last she could shake off the yoke of public service she had worn all her life and just be herself, at least sometimes.

Today was one of those times. With a precious few hours all to herself before she had to turn back into a princess in time to host a gala charity dinner tonight, she had decided to join most of the city's population at the annual agricultural fair and show. At the top of her must-see list of things were the equestrian events, starting with a demonstration by the roughriders, for which the island was renowned.

The hawker held out a silver balloon emblazoned with a bloodred rose. "I'd guess you're a rose kind of girl."

"It's pretty, but I'm more of a horse person," she said, indicating one painted with the head of a stallion. Wild of eye and mane, the picture reminded her of the native horses that roamed the hills of Nuee. The roughriders caught and tamed them for use in their daredevil performances.

"I'll make you a present of it," the hawker said on impulse. "Then you can say a man gave it to you."

She saw only sincerity in his expression. "It's kind of you, but I can't do you out of your livelihood," she insisted, fumbling in her purse for a coin. She so rarely paid for anything in cash that she knew she handled the gesture with little grace and felt annoyed with herself.

His callused hand closed around hers. "Save your money for the rest of the show. This is my treat."

"Well...thank you." She felt herself flush as she accepted the balloon, wondering why such a small gesture should touch her so deeply. If he had known who she was, she would have suspected him of trying to curry favor, but he was simply a kindly old man, spreading a bit of happiness around.

It made her even more sure that she was justified in slipping away from the palace to attend the show as an ordinary person. As a princess she rarely experienced the simple human interactions other people took for granted. When she attended events like this in her official capacity, she was escorted to the head of every line and the way was cleared for her through the crowd. She would have missed meeting the hawker altogether. Looking satisfied with his good deed, he moved away, his bouquet of balloons bobbing above his head.

"Careful, you're about to lose that."

Lost in thought, she started as another man's hand closed around hers, this time stopping her helium-filled balloon from heading skyward. The man's touch was so firm, warm and undeniably masculine that she felt herself jerk away as if strung.

"Easy, easy," he said as if he was talking to a shying horse. He let his hand drop to his side. "You seemed to be about a million miles away."

She looked at him more closely. A dark-brown jacket skimmed wide shoulders and a fit-looking body, an open-necked shirt the man's main concession to the heat. He was as tall as Adrienne's brothers, an irritant in itself, since she had always resented having to look up to meet their eyes. When she did so with the stranger, she encountered a gaze of startling blue flecked with gold and fringed by luxuriant dark lashes.

Although he was dressed as a businessman, his tanned face and hands suggested he spent a lot of time out of doors. *Rugged* was the best word to describe him, she thought, adding to herself, ruggedly handsome. His accent identified him as an American, and she wondered what brought him to the Nuee Fair as she said, "Thanks for saving my balloon."

"Why don't you try this?" Without waiting for a response, he tied the string of the balloon around her wrist. For an instant his strong fingers with their trim oval nails closed around the slender bones as if he was measuring her for a bracelet, and she felt an unaccustomed warmth surge through her. It lasted only until he released her, but she found the intensity of it oddly disquieting.

He looked up at the toy waving in the air over her head, noting the distinctive design. "You like horses, or balloons?"

"Both," she conceded, wondering why the fine hairs on the back of her neck lifted at the sound of his voice. It reminded her of dark chocolate and the stroke of velvet against her skin. Foolish, she chided herself. It must be because she was so seldom touched by anyone other than her staff that she was having such fanciful thoughts.

Above their heads a loudspeaker crackled to life with the news that the roughrider demonstration was about to start. "Are you going to watch the show?" she asked, somehow sure that he would say yes. It came to her that he looked as if he belonged in the show, rather than in the audience.

He nodded, then hesitated, as if considering an option that he wasn't sure was a good idea. "I have a pass to the members' pavilion. Would you like to see the show from there?" he asked in a rush. For some reason she felt sure that had he given himself time to think he wouldn't have issued the invitation.

As the show's royal patron she had access to any part of the fairgrounds including the members' pavilion. At least Princess Adrienne did, she reminded herself. Her alter ego, plain ordinary Dee, had no such privileges.

She was strongly tempted to accept, perhaps for the same reason that prompted him to suggest it. The sparks of awareness arcing between them were intriguing enough to warrant investigation. But it was too risky. In the members' pavilion she might run into someone she knew and her disguise was far from foolproof.

"I can't," she said, unable to conceal her reluctance. "I'm...meeting someone."

The hesitation in her voice betrayed the hastily invented excuse for what it was, and she saw his eyes take on a shuttered look. "In that case I hope you enjoy the show." He touched two fingers to his forehead in a sketchy salute and melted into the crowd.

When he had gone, she was stricken with a sudden, inexplicable sense of regret. He was only being polite in offering her the hospitality of the pavilion, she thought, and was probably thankful not to be taken up on it. All the same, she suspected she would have found the experience interesting. She sighed as she turned toward the public part of the arena.

He must be crazy, Hugh told himself as he followed the signs to the members' stand. Didn't he have enough to worry about, working with Prince Michel to establish a counterpart of his American ranch on Nuee? Hugh knew that his plans were rock solid and good for Carramer's economy, but until the ranch was a reality, he had no business letting anything sidetrack him, even a woman as intriguing as the one he'd just left.

He glanced over his shoulder. The silver balloon bobbing in the air marked her passage through the crowd surging toward the arena. She wasn't the only woman wearing a hat and dark glasses, but she was the only one who looked as if she wore them to hide behind, he thought.

Against his better judgment, he felt his curiosity stir. From her cultivated voice, she was an aristocrat, speaking English with the same refined accent as Prince Michel, as if she was a product of the best education that money could buy.

Instinct told him that her excuse about meeting someone was a brush-off. He probably wasn't to her taste, but she was too well-bred to say so. The term soured his thoughts, reminding him uncomfortably of his ex-wife. He grinned wryly to himself. If anyone had taught him the futility of chasing the unattainable, it should have been Jemima Huntly-Jordan.

He'd known when they met that Jemima Huntly was as far outside his class as diamonds were to cut glass. He should have heeded the warning signs when she lectured him on proper behavior on their first dates. But he had been a few years younger, although not enough to excuse his foolishness, and madly in love with her. He had to admit he had also been flattered that a woman like her—daughter of an ambassador, and "old money" from head to toe—could love a rancher with no family background and money so new it crackled.

What a fool he'd been, he thought. Later she'd admitted to being bored with her own social set and attracted by his no-frills attitude to life. The novelty had started to wear off almost as soon as they were married, particularly when he tried to rein in her reckless spending habits.

He hadn't expected her to live like a pauper, only to moderate her spending once in a while. Asking her to limit herself to one clothes-shopping trip to Europe a season had seemed reasonable to Hugh, but evidently not to Jemima, who acted as if he had asked her to wear rags.

"I'm a rancher, not an oil sheik," he'd reminded her, his hands full of accounts emblazoned with the crests of foreign fashion houses.

"You resent me spending money but you'll squander millions on that horse—Caravan, or whatever its name is."

"Carazzan Liberte," he'd supplied, knowing it was useless to try to explain the horse's importance to their future. Ever since his last foster father had dragged him outside and challenged him to a fist fight that had settled once and for all that Hugh wasn't as tough as he pretended, he had finally found out what he was—a rancher who belonged to the land as he belonged nowhere else.

Hugh would always be grateful to Big Dan Jordan for showing him that, and for recognizing the potential in a kid nobody else wanted. Until Dan took him in hand, Hugh had been thrown out of a string of foster homes for being uncontrollable. He bitterly regretted Dan's premature death from a heart attack and had set out to justify the faith Dan had shown in him by leaving him the land that gave him his start.

Dan had passed on to Hugh his dream of breeding the world's best riding horses. He'd known that Carazzan was the key after seeing a news story about an old horse trainer who had spotted the young stallion leading a wild herd on Nuee and had come out of retirement to catch and tame this one fantastic horse. Hugh knew how the man must have felt. He had wanted Carazzan from the moment he saw the story.

He had hardly been able to contain his excitement on hearing that Carazzan was for sale. But Jemima had drained their account of the money Hugh had set aside to buy the horse and took off to Paris with it. As a result Carazzan was bought by a member of the Carramer royal family. Maybe trying to buy the horse from them was a fool's errand, but Hugh had been a fool before and would be again. He only knew he wouldn't rest until the horse was where it belonged, in his possession.

Even so, he could have forgiven Jemima for taking the money. What he couldn't forgive was her taking another man with her then flaunting it when friends mentioned to him having seen them in each other's arms.

"It was a fling with an old flame. It means nothing," she had said when he confronted her.

It meant a lot to Hugh. Having lost the first person in the world he'd been able to trust, he couldn't believe his own wife could betray his trust without realizing the damage she'd done. He had quietly asked for a divorce, offering to take all the blame himself and to give her whatever she required for a comfortable life without him.

He had reckoned without her fury at being, as she put it, cast aside. Jemima had set out to spread rumors that his finances were in trouble, he was about to lose the ranch and he was impotent to boot. He could laugh about it now, but eighteen months ago she had nearly achieved her aim and finished him. As the baseless rumors spread, business associates began to avoid him, his credit dried up, and land he needed for expansion became mysteriously unavailable.

It had taken every ounce of street-cunning he possessed to ride out the crisis and to show the world that, not only was he not in trouble, he was prospering. Little by little, confidence in him was reestablished and he could get back to business-as-usual.

About the slurs to his manhood he could do nothing, but he had never cared what others thought of him and didn't plan to start now. After his experience with Jemima, he wasn't about to get tangled up with another woman, especially the pedigreed kind who lived in a different world from the one he inhabited.

Like the woman with the balloon, he told himself as his thoughts came full circle. He was no expert on fashion, but Jemima had taught him to recognize couture when he saw it. Although her clothes were ordinary enough, the woman with the balloon yelled couture from the top of her designer sun hat to the manicured toes of her sandal-clad feet.

She was also trouble with a capital *T,* he sensed. What was behind those big dark glasses? Every one of his survival instincts, honed while growing up in foster homes and institutions, told him she was hiding something. He would give a lot to know what it was.

He had no business even wondering, he told himself as he flashed his pass at the entrance to the members' pavilion and was ushered inside. Until that brief encounter, he'd come to the show only to check out the Nuee horses. Found nowhere else on earth, they were a spectacular hybrid of the Lipizzans that the Spaniards had brought to the island long ago and a hardy native breed. The combination had proved extraordinary, and the most extraordinary of them all was Carazzan Liberte, a stallion capable of siring the perfect riding horses Hugh dreamed of breeding.

Carazzan wasn't on show here, but he hadn't expected it any more than he would expect to run into the stallion's royal owner in the crowd. Later would do for that, when he attended a gala charity affair at the palace. He wasn't looking forward to overdosing on so much pomp and ceremony, a legacy of his misfit youth, he supposed. But attending was the only way he could get close enough to the princess to convince her that Carazzan belonged at the centerpiece of Hugh's new ranch.

A cheer went up from the crowd, and Hugh focused his attention on the arena, seeing the roughriders surge in at full gallop, stirring up clouds of dust and filling the air with their bloodcurdling cries. This was what Hugh had come to see.

Adrienne's heart picked up speed as the roughriders galloped past, crossing and recrossing one another's paths in impossibly tight formation. She knew the routines were inspired by centuries-old scenes depicted on cave walls throughout Nuee. The Mayat, ancestors of the modern-day Carramer people, had been legendary riders, training their wild horses to perform feats such as leaping from a cliff into the seething surf with a rider aboard, then carrying them safely back to the shore.

What she wouldn't give to have seen that, Adrienne admitted. The riders supposedly had no other obligations but to ride to the glory of the gods. According to legend, they had lived with their horses and sometimes died with them. Then some of the famous Lipizzans had been brought to Nuee by their Spanish owners, the native horses interbreeding with the Lipizzans over time to produce horses of spectacular beauty as well as high intelligence and ready train-ability.

The proof was in the demonstration in front of her. Fast, furious and exacting, the mock battle routines demanded split-second timing and hair-trigger reflexes. But the rough-riders and their mounts lived up to their name, and although a couple of carefully executed near-misses brought the crowd to their feet, there were no mishaps. By the time the thrilling display ended, Adrienne felt wrung out, as if she had ridden the course instead of watching it.

From force of habit she turned left out of the arena, to-ward the stables, which she made a point of visiting when-ever she attended an event at the showground in her official capacity. She realized her mistake when she rounded a cor-ner and found herself in a side alley with a cowboy barring her path. He wore a roughrider costume, but she hadn't seen him in the show. And he was drunk, she discovered as soon as he opened his mouth.

"This area's off-limits to the gen'l public," he mumbled, swaying slightly.

"My mistake," she said, backing away.

He followed her. "I'd be glad to give you a private tour."

"No, thank you, I'll just go back the way I came."

He closed the distance between them. "No hurry. No-body here but us. You like cowboys, little lady?"

His beefy hand closed around her arm, and he yanked her roughly toward him. The smell of alcohol bloomed on his breath, making her gag. "Please let me go," she said as calmly as she could, although her heart was pounding.

"Inna minute. The name's Kye. What's yours?"

"Dee," she said, still hoping she could make him see reason. The last thing she wanted was to be involved in a scene and risk having her identity discovered. "I didn't see you in the show, Kye."

"I was on this morn'n. Come on, whadda 'bout that tour? My horse is back here."

His grip on her arm was like iron as he began to tow her toward the stables. As the balloon tied to her wrist broke free and drifted away, she struggled not to panic. "I can't go with you, Kye. Someone will be looking for me soon." She lifted her voice. "I'm back here, near the stables."

The man squinted the way she'd come. "Nobody comin'."

"I'm over here," she tried again, louder this time.

"Stop that." The cowboy's free hand clamped over her mouth, reducing her cries to muffled protests. Lack of oxygen made her head start to swim. Keep calm, she willed herself. There has to be a way out of this.

Her legs almost buckled with relief when another man walked around the corner into the alley. Even more amazingly, she recognized him as the man she'd spoken to before the show. Desperately she bit down on the cowboy's hand. He yelped and loosened his grip long enough for her to say, "Over here," before her air was cut off again.

Without appearing to hurry, the man closed the distance between them, and she saw him size up the situation at a glance. But he didn't wrest her assailant off her. He simply said quietly, "What's the problem?"

"Just a little dis'greement between me and my girl," the cowboy mumbled. "Nothin' to do with anybody else."

"How about you let the lady go so she can speak for herself," the American said in the same low, controlled tone. There was no hint of threat in it, but his stance altered marginally, his assured body language suggesting that he was more than ready to back up his words with action if required.

She saw the cowboy read the same message, but he drew himself up belligerently, keeping a firm grip on his prize. "It's none of your business. She's with me." But he did remove the beefy hand covering her mouth.

Hugh glanced at her. Surely this wasn't the man she had claimed to be meeting? They seemed as ill-matched as chalk and cheese. Then he thought of himself and Jemima. "Are you with him?"

The disgusted set of her mouth gave him his answer. "I never saw him before, and if I never see him again it will be too soon."

Once again Hugh was stricken by her porcelain-doll looks. What he could see of her skin was a flawless honey-gold, and there was a hint of glossy black hair under the sun hat. It had stayed on throughout the struggle. He couldn't see her eyes behind the dark glasses but he imagined they would be as striking as what he *could* see. What in blue blazes was a woman of her apparent breeding doing, wandering around the stables of a fairground? Didn't she know it only took a few too many drinks before these cowboys fancied themselves as Don Juan?

Despite his vow not to concern himself with her, it wasn't in his nature to abandon someone who needed his help. "I said let her go." His tone suggested that he wouldn't like to have to say it a third time.

The cowboy's certainty wavered visibly. Hugh was as tall as he was, although more compactly built. Balancing lightly on the balls of his feet, he let his stance suggest— accurately—that he could take care of himself. He could almost read the cowboy's dilemma: give up the female companionship he'd anticipated or take on a fight he wasn't sure of winning. Given the woman's seductive appeal, Hugh wasn't sure which decision he would make if it were up to him. It came to him that the woman looked worth fighting for. He braced himself instinctively.

Before the cowboy could resolve his dilemma, the woman brought her knee up between his legs and connected with her target with a crunch that made Hugh wince inwardly in sympathy. With a befuddled screech, the man dropped into a spinning crouch, giving vent to a torrent of Carramer words that Hugh would bet shouldn't be used in polite company, before hobbling away toward the stables.

"I'll call security."

She couldn't let him call the authorities. It would mean too much explaining she didn't want to do. Her hand on his arm stayed him. "There's no need to call anyone, I'm all right."

"But that drunken oaf attacked you."

"Drunken is the right word. He didn't know what he was doing."

"And if he tries it with some other woman?"

Another woman might not have a white knight handy to help her, the princess admitted to herself. "I'll…I'll report it when I get home," she conceded. "He isn't going far in that condition."

"You're probably right."

He sounded reluctant to leave it there, and she got the impression he was a man who liked to see justice done. It would be, but not right now. "Thanks for coming to my rescue," she said. "How did you know I was here?"

"That silly balloon of yours. I saw it jerking around in the air from the other side of the wall."

That silly balloon as he called it just might have saved her life, she thought, and shuddered. He noticed her shudder and asked again, "Are you sure you're all right?"

She wasn't, but she made herself nod.

Hugh noticed the way her lovely long-fingered hands

were clenched together, the gesture not quite concealing how much she was trembling. He took her arm. "Come on, we're going to get you a drink."

It was a measure of her agitation that she didn't argue this time, he thought as he led her out of the alleyway and through the crowd to the members' pavilion. In the lounge, he found a quiet table in a corner and pulled out a chair for her. "What would you like to drink?"

She sank into it and rested her head on her hands. "Just coffee, thank you. I...I can't stay long."

He corralled a waiter to bring them steaming cups of the wonderfully aromatic local coffee. When it arrived, his companion seemed content to cup her hands around it, drawing comfort from the warmth.

"Feeling better now, Dee?" he asked her.

Her head came up. "What did you call me?"

"That is the name you gave the cowboy, isn't it?"

She nodded. "He said his was Kye."

"That should help you identify him for the authorities."

"Yes, of course." Making a complaint officially would involve too many awkward explanations, so she would have to find another way to make sure the cowboy was held accountable for his behavior. She was thankful when a commotion on the other side of the room saved her from further explanation. "What's going on there?"

"They're introducing Miss Show Princess to the press," he explained. "It's mentioned in the program."

The sight of so many cameras and microphones made her distinctly uneasy and she half-rose. "I should leave."

"Finish your coffee," he urged. "We're not in anyone's way."

All the same she kept her head bent toward her companion as if they were deep in conversation. Among the press she had spotted a couple of the paparazzi who made the royal family their special targets. At least their attention was on another kind of princess for the moment, she thought gratefully, wincing as flashbulbs exploded around a glamorous young woman wearing a satin sash across a traditional *leuer* gown.

"You're on edge," the American said when she jumped. "It's hardly surprising. You should have your doctor check you over when you get home."

She looked up at him, mesmerized by his brilliant gaze. He was really worried about her, she thought. Tears prickled the backs of her eyes and she put it down to her recent brush with the drunk, but knew there was more going on here. It was so rare to have someone concern themselves with her as an individual, rather than because of her position, that she was touched in spite of herself. "It's good advice."

"Then make sure you take it."

Another flashbulb popped, close to them this time. Miss Show Princess and her entourage had moved across the room to take advantage of the panoramic view of the fairgrounds beyond the lounge windows. It brought them to within a few feet of Adrienne's table. Shaken, she pushed her chair back. "I really must go."

The American moved to her side to help her up but was jostled by one of the photographers, throwing him against Adrienne. Instinctively he reached for her, steadying her. Anyone might have done the same, but she was stunned by the eddies of awareness the contact set up in her. She put it down to her heightened vulnerability after her encounter with the cowboy, but that hardly accounted for the strength of her response. She looked up at the American in confusion.

At that moment another flashbulb popped, then a whole barrage of them as Miss Show Princess paraded for the cameras. Adrienne used the moment to slip away toward the door, aware that the American was close behind her. "There's no need to leave on my account," she insisted.

"I only came for the equestrian events," he said. "I'll see you home."

"No." The word came out more forcefully than she intended, and she saw his expression turn cold. After he had done so much for her, she hadn't meant it to sound so much like a dismissal, but she could see he had taken it as one. "I mean, my car's parked right outside."

"Then I'll see you to your car," he said coolly.

Thankfully, she had borrowed an unpretentious sedan from her assistant, who knew about her little adventures. Her staff might not approve, but their loyalty to her ensured that they helped her and kept her secret. "Thank you for everything," she said as she got in. He nodded.

He watched as she maneuvered the small car out of the tight space and drove off. About to turn away, he spotted a flash of crimson on the ground. Her scarf must have caught in the door and been pulled off when she closed it.

He picked it up, and a faint whiff of her scent teased his nostrils—richly floral, like a balmy tropical evening, he thought. He tucked it into his jacket pocket. Nuee was a small island. It wouldn't hurt to hang on to the scarf in case they met again.

Chapter Two

In response to a direct tap on her dressing room door, Adrienne said, "Come in."

It was her personal assistant, Cindy Cook. The leather-bound file she carried under her arm made an interesting contrast with her pale-blue ball gown. She bobbed a curtsy then stopped short. "You look wonderful, Your Highness."

Cindy had worked for the princess since they graduated from university together, so she wasn't given to flattery for its own sake. Adrienne felt pleased that her new gown had made such a strong impression.

It was a glorious emerald-green, the color being one reason Adrienne had fallen in love with it; the design was another. From the front it looked like a stylish sheath that outlined her slender curves before fanning into a miniature train at her feet.

The back was a different matter. Cut almost to the waist, the dress was supported by a web of shoestring straps criss-crossing her bare back. With her glossy black hair swirled into a mass of curls high on her head and set off by an emerald tiara, she looked every inch the royal princess, she knew. Her alter ego, Dee, was nowhere to be seen.

"You don't think it's too daring for a charity affair?" she asked Cindy.

"The photographers will love it."

As an answer it was a clever evasion, Adrienne recognized. It probably *was* overly daring but it was too late for her to change now. In any case, she was in the mood to cause a stir tonight and wondered if it was an aftereffect of her bad experience at the show. She hadn't told Cindy about the cowboy or the man who had come to her rescue, telling herself no lasting harm had been done. But had it? She felt so fragile that she couldn't be sure. She couldn't even report the incident to anyone without revealing that she had gone out incognito.

"The dress is by an Australian designer, Aloys Gada. Allie recommended him," she told Cindy.

Allie, or more precisely Her Highness, Princess Alison, was Lorne's Australian wife. With her egalitarian ideals, she was like a breath of fresh air in the royal family. So was Caroline, the American woman Michel had married, Adrienne thought, smiling to herself as she recalled how Michel had been betrothed to Caroline's twin sister in an ancient ceremony when they were children. They hadn't expected to be held to the contract when they grew up, and it was Caroline that Michel really loved. But it had worked out well in the end, when Caroline's twin schemed to get them back together. Like Lorne and Allie, Caroline and Michel were blissfully happy, and Adrienne couldn't wait to become an aunt to their child in a few months' time.

"What are you thinking about? I'll bet it isn't tonight's affair," Cindy guessed, watching her royal employer.

Adrienne drew herself back to the present. For a moment she had let herself fantasize about being happily married like her brothers, with a husband to admire her appearance instead of a paid assistant. Cindy was supportive, but it wasn't the same, somehow. "I was thinking of someone I met today," she confessed.

The cowboy she dismissed as being of no consequence, a drunk who didn't know any better. The American was another matter. He haunted her thoughts in a way that disturbed her for some reason.

Cindy's face dimpled into a smile. "A man?"

"They do comprise half of the universe."

"Not this universe."

In spite of herself, Adrienne sighed, knowing Cindy was right. Before her assistant could ask about the man occupying her thoughts, Adrienne said, "We'd better get down to business. Who are the important names on the guest list tonight?"

Opening her file, Cindy reeled off a list of mostly elderly local nobles. Adrienne nodded. "No surprises there." Since tonight's gala was in recognition of donations to the children's charity she chaired, the princess knew most of the major benefactors already. It promised to be a dull evening, but she could endure it for the sake of the orphans, she told herself. "Any new faces?"

"Anyone young, you mean?"

Cindy knew her too well. "It would make a pleasant change."

Cindy scanned the list. "Hardly anyone our age. The youngest is a thirty-something foreigner, a Mr. Hugh Jordan, here to finalize an investment project with Prince Michel."

Adrienne felt a jolt and wondered at its source. "Is that why he got an invitation?"

Cindy shook her head. "My note says he was the largest single donor to the appeal."

"No doubt he thinks the donation makes him look like a big man in Michel's eyes." She had recognized the man's name as soon as Cindy said it. Hugh Jordan planned to establish a vast ranch north of Nuee City, on land that Adrienne had wanted for the same reason.

It still rankled that her brother was more willing to trust a foreigner with the project and the boost it would give to Nuee's economy than Adrienne herself. She knew as much about breeding horses as any man. But she was a princess and princesses didn't do that sort of thing, she thought angrily, recalling Michel's reasoned response.

He hadn't used those exact words, preferring ones like *inappropriate* and *taking up too much of your valuable time,* but the end result was the same. Hugh Jordan got to do what an accident of birth prevented her from doing.

It seemed Michel had told the man about her interest in horse breeding, particularly the Nuee saddlebreds, and he had asked to meet her. But she told her brother she had no intention of sharing her hard-won expertise with the stranger so he could enjoy all the benefits.

Michel had thought her response petty. He was probably right but she didn't care. Now Hugh Jordan had finagled his way into her charity dinner, anyway. His donation to the appeal was so substantial that there was no way she could avoid meeting him tonight.

"I'll bet Hugh Jordan smokes cigars and only talks about price movements on the stock exchange. And he's probably this big," Cindy said.

As her assistant pantomimed a huge girth, Adrienne was forced to laugh. "And no matter how stuffy or boring he is, you'll charm him into giving an even larger donation to your beloved children," Cindy added more seriously.

Adrienne let her eyes flash acceptance of the challenge. "I'll consider it a personal obligation."

Cindy dealt with the rest of the details in her usual efficient way, then closed the file. "That's everything you need to know for now." Adrienne stood up and felt herself sway slightly. Cindy looked concerned. "Are you all right? Perhaps you overdid things by going out this afternoon."

Adrienne heard the disapproval in Cindy's voice. Her assistant made no secret of disliking her employer's habit of going out incognito, even though she had lent the princess her own car for the purpose.

"I'm fine. I probably just need to eat something before I go down."

"I'll have a tray sent up right away."

She was as good as her word, but Adrienne couldn't bring herself to eat much before she made her entrance into the ballroom. She took her place at the head of the room as the orchestra played the Carramer national anthem, "From Sea to Stars." No matter how many times she heard it the music still stirred her blood.

As her experienced staff organized a receiving line, Cindy moved to Adrienne's side ready to discreetly prompt the princess with any names and personal details she might need. She wasn't needed a great deal. Adrienne considered herself lucky in having a good memory, and now she greeted each person by name, asking after their partners, children and any other concerns that came to mind.

Then she felt herself go cold from head to foot.

"Mr. Hugh Jordan, rancher from San Francisco," Cindy murmured, thinking Adrienne's hesitation meant she needed help identifying the next guest.

"Your Highness, this is indeed a surprise," the man said, his rich, deep voice laced with irony. From the glitter in his remarkable blue eyes, Adrienne gathered that the surprise wasn't any more pleasant for him than it was for her.

Far from being the paunchy, stuffy businessman she and

Cindy had envisioned, Hugh Jordan was tall, muscular and undeniably good-looking. Even in the relative anonymity of a tuxedo, she recognized him instantly. Mr. Hugh Jordan, rancher from San Francisco, was the man who had come to her rescue at the fair.

Like the other guests he touched her hand in a token handshake, but instead of releasing her immediately as protocol required, his strong fingers curled into her palm and a shiver ran through her. "Small world, isn't it," he said softly.

Only years of royal training enabled her to keep a bright smile on her face, although her features felt as if they might crack at any moment. "It's a pleasure to meet you, Mr. Jordan." Her heart was beating so rapidly that she felt lightheaded, but not by so much as a flicker of an eyelash did she let herself acknowledge their previous meeting.

For a fleeting moment a shadow of a doubt crossed his face, and she saw him mentally comparing the princess in front of him with the woman he'd encountered earlier. In her designer gown with her hair expertly dressed and a fortune in diamonds and emeralds adorning her head, neck and earlobes, she knew she looked very different from the woman he'd met earlier. Could she convince him it was a case of mistaken identity?

Then he returned his gaze to her face and his eyes hardened. She felt her heart sink. Convincing a man like Hugh Jordan that he was wrong wasn't an option, she saw.

"The pleasure is mine, Your Highness," he said in a tone so smooth and hard it reminded her of volcanic glass. "I look forward to spending some time later this evening discussing our...mutual interests."

Before she could summon her voice to reply, he released her hand and moved on, forcing her to deal with the next guest and giving her no time to collect herself. Only part of her mind was on her duty, she found. What did he mean—discuss their mutual interests? He had come to Carramer to negotiate setting up a ranch on Nuee, the ranch she herself had wanted to establish. If the American thought he could take advantage of their earlier encounter to involve her in his project against her will, he was in for a disappointment.

The idea was so distasteful that she rejected it instinctively. She recognized an element of wishful thinking in the hope that he wasn't the type to do such a thing. Just because he had come to her rescue didn't necessarily mean he wouldn't use it to get something he wanted. Her position made her an ideal target, she knew.

Hugh Jordan had stumbled on a secret known only to her immediate staff. How would he use the information? The question nagged at her all through the ritual of predinner drinks. Usually she enjoyed circulating among her guests, showing her appreciation for their generous support of the children's charity. Tonight she was so agitated that Cindy put a hand on her arm and steered her aside.

"Are you feeling all right, Your Highness?"

"What makes you ask?"

"You're on your second glass of champagne already. That isn't like you at all, especially when you've eaten so little."

Adrienne looked at the goblet in her hand, surprised to find it almost drained. She had drunk it without being conscious of it. Cindy was right. Usually she restricted herself to mineral water before meals and a single glass of wine at dinner. "Thanks for noticing. I guess I'm a little distracted tonight." Shaken, she handed the glass to Cindy.

Her assistant set it aside. "You looked a bit shell-shocked when I introduced Hugh Jordan. Do you know him?"

"Tonight was the first time we've been introduced."

Cindy accepted the literal truth without question. "Just as well, because as the appeal's largest donor, he's seated on your right at dinner. He'll be coming to escort you in at any minute."

Adrienne's gaze was drawn irresistibly to the man who captured her attention even across the considerable expanse of the ballroom. Again her heart started its uncomfortably fast beating at the sight of him. Wearing hand-tailored evening clothes, he managed to look more like one of the cold-eyed lawmen she'd seen in films about the American West. He was a head taller than most of the other male guests, and she saw him methodically scan the crowd until he located his quarry—her.

He started toward her like an aimed bullet, the crowd making way for him as if Hugh and not Adrienne had been royalty. She sensed his disapproval from a dozen feet away, and it cut through her like a knife. "Is there time to change the seating arrangements?" she asked Cindy in a low voice.

Cindy checked her watch. "We're due to sit down in four minutes. I'd have to ask the kitchen staff to delay serving dinner while I reshuffle the seating." She sounded frayed and Adrienne knew if anyone else had suggested it, her assistant would have told them what she thought in no uncertain terms.

"Don't bother, then, everything will be fine," she assured her assistant. It wasn't fair to burden her with a problem Adrienne had to admit was of her own making. She lifted her head and fixed her best princess-smile to her face as the source of her tension reached her side. "Mr. Jordan, I'm told we're to be dinner partners."

He offered her his bent arm, and she was proud of hesitating only fractionally as she tucked her hand into it. "All

things considered, you should call me Hugh," he growled.
"I already know the name you prefer to answer to."

She knew he was referring to Dee, the name he had heard
her use at the fair. "My name is Adrienne," she said firmly,
wishing she wasn't bound by the rules of etiquette to keep
her hand in his arm when every instinct urged her to tear
herself free and run as fast as she could away from him.

The banquet table was large enough to land a small plane
on, but with Hugh at her side she felt as if it was barely
roomy enough for the two of them. "What brings you to
Nuee, Hugh?" she made herself ask in a conversational
tone, as the first course was served with the precision of a
military operation.

"I'm sure your staff briefed you on why I'm here. But
for the record, I plan to establish a ranch north of Nuee
City and breed saddle horses. It'll be the South Pacific
counterpart of a similar facility I own back in the States."

As the governor of the islands of Isle des Anges and
Nuee, her brother, Prince Michel, had to give royal assent
before a foreigner could make an investment on that scale
in Carramer, she knew. Perhaps it wasn't too late to convince Michel to change his mind. "How far advanced are
your plans?" she asked.

"Far enough. The land is already mine through a Car-
ramer-based holding company. All I need now is royal approval to set up the ranch."

Approval her brother had withheld from his own sister,
she reminded herself, feeling her anger rise. "I suppose you
want me to put in a good word for you with Michel," she
said, her tone unconsciously harsh.

He took a sip of the excellent French wine she had refused in favor of mineral water. "I should think you'd be
more worried about what I might say to the prince than
what you should say to him," he said.

She was uncomfortably sure that she knew exactly what he was suggesting but she decided to make him spell it out. "I can't imagine what you mean."

He glanced around, but the guests nearest to them were engrossed in conversation and enjoying the seafood course that had been placed before them. "You know exactly what I mean...Dee."

So he did intend to take advantage of what he had learned about her activities. Her spirits plummeted. "Kindly don't call me that here," she said, keeping defeat out of her voice with an effort. She hadn't known quite how much she valued her vacations from duty until they were under threat.

"I gather no one knows about your little foray but you and me."

"My personal staff know that I like to...keep in touch," she said awkwardly.

"Is that what you call risking your beautiful neck for a few thrills?"

She drew herself up regally. "You presume a lot on very little knowledge, Mr. Jordan."

His hand slid over hers in a fleeting but oddly possessive gesture. "It's a bad habit of mine, especially with a lady whose beautiful a— anatomy I've had the pleasure of saving."

"Crudely put but accurate," she snapped. "Why do I sense that a simple thank-you isn't enough to persuade you to drop the subject?"

"Because it won't be," he said so mildly that it hardly sounded like a threat at all. More a promise, she thought. Men like Hugh Jordan didn't threaten. "Why did you refuse me when I asked for a meeting?"

"I didn't—"

"Oh, the princes' office gave me the official excuses, but

in my experience we can generally do the things we most want to do. Therefore, you wouldn't see me because you didn't want to.''

It was bad enough being cut off in midsentence. Of the many people in her life, perhaps only her brothers would have dared. ''Royalty has its obligations,'' she said, annoyed at being second-guessed so accurately.

''Then Nuee's prosperity should be high on the list.''

''Of course it is. It's the smallest of Carramer's main islands with the least resources.''

''One of them being native horses with the potential to be the world's greatest saddlebreds.''

''Agreed,'' she said.

''So why put up a fight?''

''Because I refused a meeting?''

His eyes gleamed. ''A confession, princess?''

Too late, she saw the trap. ''A question...and you haven't answered it.''

He spread his long fingers wide. ''Your brother tells me you're the greatest living expert on Nuee's native horses. With your expertise and my setup, we could conquer the riding world.''

''Why not the other way around?'' she said softly.

His breath hissed between those inviting full lips. ''So that's what this is all about. You wanted that land for yourself, didn't you?''

''It's perfect for raising saddlebreds.''

''So why didn't you buy it?'' He swept a gaze around the banquet hall. He knew the value of the silverware alone would feed a normal family for a year. ''It can't be lack of money.''

''Try lack of a Y chromosome.''

He looked startled, as if the idea would never occur to him. ''Because you're female? Carramer isn't that feudal.''

"It depends on one's family."

"Your brothers?" When she nodded, he said, "They must have good reason for keeping you out of the ranching business. Maybe they're trying to protect you."

"Spoken like a typical male," she said. "I can take care of myself."

"The way you did this afternoon? What's with you, anyway, princess? You could have been injured or killed sneaking out like that."

She let her eyes flash regal fire at him and waited for him to quail. When he didn't, she snapped, "I would have handled that drunken oaf. I did handle him, come to think of it." She saw Hugh wince at the memory of her well-aimed kick. "And I never sneak."

"So this isn't the first time you've gone out alone and in disguise." It wasn't a question. It was certainty. He didn't seem surprised when she didn't deny it and went on in an angry voice, "Princess, it seems to me that you don't know when you're well-off."

Confusion gripped her. She had feared he would use what he knew to gain some benefit, but instead he sounded angry on her account. This was getting much too personal. Luckily the next course was being brought in. "I'm glad we had this talk, Hugh, but I can't monopolize you all evening."

He knew a dismissal when he heard one. He might be a self-made man but his education, rough as it was, had included the rules of etiquette. Both of them owed some of their attention to the guests on either side of them. "There's still my dance," he reminded the princess before she could turn to the man on her left. He had the satisfaction of seeing her lovely eyes widen.

"Your dance?"

"As your appeal's biggest benefactor, I get to dance with the princess at least once tonight."

"I may retire early."

"Even you wouldn't buck the system that far."

He was right, damn him. She still had a feeling he wanted something from her, something he hadn't mentioned yet. She resolved to make it a short dance. "Very well, then, we'll continue this later."

He nodded graciously enough but muttered something that sounded like, "You bet we will." With a resigned sigh, she turned her attention to the man seated on her left. He was a meteorologist, she remembered from Cindy's briefing. She hoped discussing the weather would be easier on her blood pressure than talking with Hugh.

Even with her attention directed elsewhere she was aware of him, she noticed uncomfortably. As her companion launched into a long dissertation about the effects of the various currents on Carramer's water temperatures, she nibbled around the edges of her food, mostly pushing it around her plate to give the appearance of eating.

When the lecture faltered, she dragged a snippet of information out of her memory. "I believe you're also interested in the thermal mapping of tropical storms."

The meteorologist colored with pleasure. "Your Highness is well informed."

Efficient, too, in studying the briefing notes Cindy had prepared for her ahead of time. Adrienne inclined her head. "It's kind of you to say so. Please, go on."

This started a fresh wave of information that she absorbed with only half her attention. The other half kept shifting to Hugh who had his head bent close to a middle-aged blond woman on his right. Had Cindy mentioned her? She was somebody's wife, Adrienne recalled, although right now she wasn't acting much like one.

The woman was all but batting her eyes at him. Hugh didn't seem to mind, lapping up the attention like mother's milk. She wasn't jealous. The woman was welcome to him, Adrienne told herself. He annoyed her, and not only because he knew her secret. He refused to treat her with the deference due her position, challenging and insulting her in a way no one else dared to do.

In fairness she couldn't blame him for securing the land she had wanted for herself. That fault lay with her brother. But she did resent Hugh's ready acceptance of it as his right, and his attitude that, as a woman and a princess, she needed protecting from the big, bad world.

All the same he intrigued her, possibly because she didn't intimidate him. America had no royal family, she recalled, having shed their ties with their monarch centuries before. Yet Hugh's attitude didn't seem to come from lack of experience with royalty as much as from the depths of his own character. He would bow before anyone who had earned his deference, but not otherwise, she sensed.

The thought of dancing with him was scary and exhilarating by turns.

At the end of the elaborate meal she stood up, signaling a return to the ballroom, where her heart started to flutter in anticipation. Surely she couldn't want to dance with Hugh Jordan? If he passed on what he knew, he could cause trouble for her with her brothers. By right she should keep as far away from him as possible. Yet her eyes sought him out with the same recklessness that sent a moth darting to a fatal flame.

"May I have this dance, Your Highness?" he asked formally as the orchestra struck up a waltz.

"Yes." Strange how hard it was to force the single word out.

With a smoothness she hadn't expected, he took her hand

in his and led her into the center of the room. Pressing against the small of her back, his other hand felt fiery, the almost-backless dress no shield against his touch. She was relieved when they completed the obligatory circle of the room and other dancers joined them on the floor. Alone with Hugh in the spotlight, she had felt exposed and vulnerable.

"You look surprised that I can dance," he murmured, his lips close to her ear. "Did you doubt that the foreign cowboy had it in him?"

His breath ruffled her hair, distracting her. "You obviously know your way around a banquet hall and a dance floor, and you're smart enough in business to impress Michel. So why pretend you're a hick cowboy?"

"Because it's what I am. A street kid, a foundling, call it what you like. I wasn't born with your advantages."

She tensed involuntarily. "You mean belonging to the royal family?"

"I mean belonging to *any* family. I didn't have a family until I was fourteen years old, but you have since birth. Maybe that's why you don't appreciate it."

His harsh tone made her wince almost more than the grip on her hand which had tightened as he spoke. "What makes you think I don't?"

"Why else would you run away from everything you are for the sake of a cheap thrill or two?"

"You could never understand," she said bitterly.

"I'm not sure I want to, princess."

"Must you keep calling me that?"

The corners of his mouth lifted slightly. "Would you prefer Dee?"

"I'd prefer you let me go. We've done our duty now and...oh."

She felt herself sway, held upright only by his arm around her. "Are you okay?"

"Just a little lightheaded. I'll be fine if I can get some air."

Still half supporting her, he led her through a set of French doors opening onto a wide terrace lit by flaming torches. By their flickering light he found a stone bench and pressed her onto it. "You didn't eat much in there, did you?"

"A little."

"And I'll bet you didn't see a doctor when you got back, either." Her look gave him his answer. "Don't you realize you could be in shock after what happened at the show?"

"But I'm not," she insisted.

To her chagrin, his strong fingers pried her eyelids up one after the other and he inspected her pupils as he might have done a horse he intended buying at auction. "Your eyes are clear and your color is good. Next time eat a little more before hitting the dance floor."

She was tempted to remind him whose fault it was she was there in the first place, but she was too distracted by the feel of his palm against the side of her face and had to fight a stupid inclination to lean into it. "I'm just tired," she ventured.

"And willful and dangerously reckless," he added. "At one time I'd have given my right arm for a brother who cared about me as much as yours do, and you don't have the sense to appreciate them."

No one had ever spoken to her so bluntly, not even her brothers. She drew herself up shakily. "Kindly remember to whom you are speaking."

"I haven't forgotten," he said softly, touching a finger to her chin and tilting her face up a fraction more. "It's the only thing stopping me from doing what I wanted to do this afternoon at the show.''

She could hardly speak. ''What's that?''

''Kiss you senseless.''

Her breath snagged in her throat as she felt her arousal build. It seemed inconceivable that Hugh could have such an effect on her with a few words and a touch, but he had. ''You don't even know me.''

He shrugged dismissively. ''Call it chemistry, but it's the way I feel. I spent most of the time between the show and coming here wondering how to find you again.''

''And now that you have?''

He glanced around but the others were still dancing. They had the terrace to themselves. ''I find you're so far above me that I can't reach high enough to touch you.''

''Are you sure?'' She stood up so their faces were as close to level as his extra inches in height would allow. Her stiletto-heeled shoes didn't help nearly enough.

It was all the invitation he needed. With an indrawn breath he slid his arms around her and found her mouth. His lips were as commanding as she'd imagined, shaping hers to some hidden agenda of his own.

There was nothing hesitant in the way he gathered her against him and merged his mouth with hers. His hand slid to the back of her neck, pressing her closer, letting her feel his body heat as the rich masculine taste of him filled her mouth.

If she'd thought she was aroused before, it was nothing compared to the fire racing through her by the time he released her. She felt so shaken that it was an effort to slip her mask of royal reserve back into place. ''Satisfied now?''

He seemed far less moved by the kiss than she was, and the discovery rankled for some reason.

"Let's say it's a start."

"It can't be any such thing," she said haughtily. "This is insane. If I was feeling better…"

"You'd do exactly what we just did," he supplied with infuriating coolness. "You wanted to kiss me as much as I wanted to kiss you."

But in his case it meant a lot less, she saw. Wanting to hit back, she said, "It's done now. Over."

Slowly he shook his head. "Oh, no, princess, it isn't over by a long shot. There's still the matter of your reckless behavior to be discussed, and another matter I intended to bring up with you."

"What's that?" she asked suspiciously.

"It will keep. Right now, you should rest—and have your doctor take a look at you."

"Anything else?"

"Yes, how soon can I see you again?"

As soon as she heard herself ask the question she cursed his ability to throw her off balance, for she—

Chapter Three

As soon as he heard himself ask the question, Hugh recognized his mistake. He needed to meet the princess again if he was to persuade her to sell Carazzan to him, but he hadn't meant to sound as if he wanted to see her again for her own sake.

The problem was he did, he thought with an inward sigh of frustration. She'd brought him face-to-face with something he hadn't thought about in a long while—how much time he spent alone. Granted, it was from choice. He was well aware that he had no need to spend even one night alone unless he wanted to. He usually wanted to. This felt different. And dangerous.

"I'm hosting a session for the Children's Right to Ride organization at my country house the day after tomorrow. You're welcome to join us," she said, breaking into his thoughts. Her voice sounded brittle, as if she, too, questioned the wisdom of another meeting even as she set it up.

He already knew that Right to Ride was the Carramer equivalent of the various riding for the disabled groups he supported back home. He was a big fan of the benefits horse riding provided to people with disabilities but hadn't expected someone like the princess to share his passion. Maybe negotiating with her wasn't going to be such a battle after all.

It wasn't as hard as he expected to picture her helping children with problems. This whole lavish evening had been on their account, he recalled. He hoped it was because she cared about the children and not only because it was her royal duty. There was one way to find out.

"I'll be there."

"I'll have an invitation sent to your hotel."

She might have known he would be punctual. Cindy had found out where he was staying and issued the invitation. Cindy knew everything, except why Adrienne felt so strongly attracted to the last man who should interest her. Adrienne told herself she wanted to see him to ensure that Hugh kept her secret, but there was more to it.

With a worrying prescience, she knew he was there before he joined her at the white railing as she watched several children with varying degrees of disability being introduced to the thrill of riding. They were under the supervision of skilled therapists, with teams of side walkers to ensure their safety, but to the children all that mattered was the experience of being on a horse.

Hugh greeted her formally, as if the kiss had never happened. The kiss that had left her mouth swollen, the feel of his hand branded on her nape. She didn't know whether she was relieved or annoyed. He was the white knight type, she sensed, and she'd had her fill of white knights in her two brothers. She was ready to show them, and any other candidates for the role of protector, that she didn't need them. She could look out for herself.

All the same, when the tall, rangy American smiled a greeting at her and her gaze settled on his generous mouth, she felt a surge of response deep inside. It had nothing to do with needing a man to protect or save her, and everything to do with needing one to love her, she thought, feeling her mood notch downward.

Count your blessings, she told herself sternly. How could she let her petty problems depress her when others had so much more to worry about? "Look at that little girl," she said, as much to herself as to Hugh. "With such limited use of her legs, she has to do all the work with her arms, but she's having the time of her life."

"It's also helping her a great deal," he added, thinking of similar sessions he had organized at his own ranch. "I recall seeing a tape showing how the steps a horse takes involve the same muscles and joints that humans use. Put someone with restricted movement capability on a horse and they get to feel what normal movement is like for the first time."

"It's a lot more fun than other kinds of therapy," she commented.

He saw her lovely features twist into a grimace. "That sounds like the voice of experience."

She nodded. "When I was fourteen, I broke my ankle when my horse rolled on me. After spending weeks in a cast, I needed physiotherapy to get full movement back and be able to ride again. It was pure hell."

"I know what you mean. As a kid I had my share of broken bones, too."

"Was it a horse-riding accident for you, too?"

A shadow darkened his features. "I wasn't that lucky."

She waited for him to elaborate. When he didn't, she was left to wonder about the bleak look she glimpsed in his eyes before he turned his head away. At the gala, he had mentioned growing up without a family. Losing her parents had been the worst experience of her life, but at least she had their memory and her brothers' love. She might chafe against their overprotectiveness, but she couldn't imagine what it would be like not to have their love and support through thick and thin. Had Hugh suffered from being alone, possibly even physically?

She had a feeling Hugh wouldn't welcome her sympathy, so she returned her attention to the riders, hoping he would think that her blurred vision was on their account. A little boy was being lifted from a wheelchair onto a horse. As he saw the world from above people's heads for the first time, his small features glowed with delight.

"In our program we had one who couldn't see," Hugh said, a burr in his voice. "Somehow the horse knew to let her touch him from head to toe. He never moved a muscle."

"They're amazing that way."

Amazing was the word she would use for how she felt right now. The Right to Ride movement was her favorite cause, but the sudden heightening of her emotions had little to do with the children and everything to do with the man beside her. With one foot anchored on the bottom railing and both arms looped over the top one, he looked to be in his element. "The children or the horses?" she asked in an attempt to keep her feelings where they belonged.

"Both. Whenever I host sessions for a similar organization in America, I'm awed by the courage of the children who achieve so much against horrendous odds. I'm also struck by how the horses always know to be gentle with them."

He had summed up her feelings exactly. Somehow she hadn't expected such empathy from him. It felt wonderful and dangerous, she sensed, as if it brought them closer than was wise. Nevertheless she found herself turning to him to ask, "Would you like to look around?"

"If you have the time." It was the opening he'd hoped for. Today she wasn't suffering possible shock, and he wasn't distracted by a body sculpted in heaven in a dress that was barely there. Or so he told himself, not sure how convincingly.

Today the princess wore riding clothes, expensively tailored so they skimmed her slender curves like a second skin. Her cream long-sleeved shirt was buttoned nearly to the neck, concealing more than it revealed. It didn't stop his imagination from running riot as she walked ahead of him toward the stables.

Her movements were as graceful as a gazelle's. He could easily imagine her riding like the wind with her glorious raven hair streaming like a banner behind her. He liked the way she wore it down today, caught by some kind of bear claw thing made of tortoiseshell. It lifted her hair away from her classical features and swanlike neck, allowing most of it to stream down her back where it rippled like satin in the light breeze.

With an effort he focused on why he was here. Somehow he had to convince her to sell him Carazzan. It was going to be an uphill job, he had no doubt. If their roles had been reversed, no offer on earth would have made him part with the horse, yet he expected her to do it. They reached a stable with Carrazan's name beside the door. Mentally he braced himself.

However, she walked past it to a second stable. Hugh made himself bide his time and was glad he had when he found himself in a setup fit for a string of royal horses. Most were a hybrid crossing of the fabled Nuee native horse, he assessed from the finely chiseled heads appearing at each stall as they passed, the large expressive eyes inspecting him as curiously as he studied them.

Without needing to check, he knew that these superb creatures would have short, level backs, clean, straight legs with long, sloping pasterns and well-formed feet. Most were roan, golden or bay like their ancestors, and were likely to be every bit as hardy, sure-footed and intelligent.

If they were the result of the princess's breeding program, Hugh's respect for her skill needed adjusting a long way upward. His heartbeat quickened. What couldn't he do with these beauties and a horse like Carazzan?

Adrienne noticed his silence. "What do you think?"

"I think you're doing amazing work, Your Highness."

Her finely penciled eyebrow canted upward. "Titles now, Hugh? You must be impressed."

"I'm happy to give credit where it's due," he said mildly. "These are some of the finest horses I've seen in a long time."

She released a sigh. "Coming from you, that's a compliment."

"Why from me?"

"Your reputation as a breeder, the success your horses have achieved in endurance events, the show ring, even the Olympics. It's an impressive record."

"But not impressive enough for you to roll out the red carpet for me," he guessed.

She smiled wryly. "Red carpets are supposed to be my act."

And so was the land he'd purchased north of the city. "If I hadn't bought the land, some other outsider would have bought it and done exactly what I plan to do," he said, recalling the reason for her antipathy toward him. "Prince Michel is keen to attract more foreign investment to Nuee."

Her expression darkened. "We both know it isn't the main reason why he wants you to set up the ranch."

"I'm not going to apologize for being male."

It would be a sin against nature if he did. "You don't have to. This is Michel's doing, not yours."

He held up a hand. "Now stop right there, princess. You make me sound like some kind of puppet for your brother. He may govern the island, but he doesn't govern me. If I wanted to, say, take on a female partner, I wouldn't need to consult him first."

Her heart leaped. Was Hugh saying what she thought he was saying? "You'd actually consider a partnership?" she asked, keeping the hope out of her voice with an effort.

He hadn't considered it until this precise moment, but now it struck him as a possible solution to his dilemma. Considering how badly she seemed to want to be part of the new operation, she might agree to sell him Carazzan in return for a stake in it. "I might, if I decide it will benefit the ranch," he said slowly, thinking it through as he spoke. "I can't be here all the time. I have good managers, but I still need to pay some attention to my operation in the states. Having someone who knows what they're doing to oversee things here would be a smart idea."

She ran a gentle hand over the muzzle of the nearest horse, and it whickered softly in appreciation. If she touched him like that, he'd whicker, too, Hugh thought as a surge of heat infused his body. His concentration wavered until he brought himself under control with an effort.

As if sensing his discomfort, she let her hand drop. "Why did you choose Nuee?"

"It's ideal horse country, as you well know." He didn't add that Carazzan's presence on the island had played a big part in his choice of where to expand next. "The climate's a lot more forgiving, too. Back home we needed to build a thirty-five-thousand-square-foot indoor stable and arena so we could run our programs year-round. I can't see a need for heated barns or an indoor arena here.''

"Not unless you're planning trail rides to Mount Mayat.'' She smiled, thinking of Nuee's balmy year-round temperatures that rarely varied by more than seven degrees between summer and winter. Even at the summit of the mountain, the lowest temperature ever recorded was not quite down to freezing, when it had snowed briefly.

"Do you recommend it?''

"The view is spectacular.''

"I'll be sure and check it out while I'm here, if you know where I can get a reliable mount.''

As he'd hoped when he made the request, she said, "My stables are at your disposal.''

He wondered how she would react if he suggested riding Carazzan. One step at a time, he told himself. It pained him to think of giving up even part of his new facility to the princess, when everything in him warned against getting involved with her. She was cut from the same cloth as his ex-wife, the very person who had cost him Carazzan, he reminded himself. He was probably crazy to consider jumping into bed with an even more blue-blooded woman to get the horse back.

He frowned inwardly. Partners were often described as being in bed together, but he would need to think of another metaphor for him and the princess. The heat simmering inside him, undermining his self-control, made the idea of being in bed with Adrienne appealing, but it was also foolhardy in the extreme. Hadn't he learned anything from his experience with Jemima?

He wasn't being entirely fair to the princess, dangling a partnership in front of her when she had no idea of his price, he thought. When she found out, he probably wouldn't have to worry about being in bed with her, because it was the last thing she would want from him. She might even have Prince Lorne reverse the law making it illegal to throw foreigners off the top of Mount Mayat. According to Hugh's reading, centuries ago it had been a popular treatment meted out to foreigners who offended the royal family.

Adrienne's thoughts whirled. Becoming a partner in Hugh's ranch was a huge compromise, she knew, but surely it was better than being shut out of her dream entirely? Perhaps Hugh would tire of the ranch once it was established. As his partner she would be the logical person to take it over, and by then she would have proved to her brothers that she could handle it. She reached a sudden decision. "I'd like to show you something special."

He guessed what she was going to show him, and his insides twisted in anticipation. But fairness made him say, "I don't want to keep you from your guests."

She shook her head. "I mainly provide the horses and the facilities. Sometimes I fill in as a side walker but today they have more volunteers than they need, so I can slip away for a while."

It was hard not to hold his breath as the princess led him through a side door into the adjoining stable. At last. He could hear the stallion snorting long before they reached his stall. He could scent a stranger about and was telling Hugh in no uncertain terms that this was his territory.

Hugh knew how the horse felt. He experienced the same fever of possession whenever he walked over his new land. He wasn't sure he could give up even part of it to Adrienne. Then he caught sight of the stallion and knew it would be worth any pain, even sharing his dream, if it meant possessing such a horse.

"Carazzan Liberte," he breathed as flames of longing

raced through his veins. The need to caress the long, arched neck and swing himself aboard the strong back and urge Carazzan into the spectacular prancing gait that characterized his breed was almost unbearable. This horse should have been in Hugh's stable, quivering under his hand as he ran it along the stallion's shining flank. He felt a surge of anger toward his ex-wife for denying him the opportunity and, irrationally, toward Adrienne because his loss had been her gain.

Adrienne shot him a curious look. "You know of Carazzan?"

He took a deep breath. "But for a personal problem, I was going to buy him and make him the centerpiece of my breeding program."

"He's still the centerpiece of mine." Suspicion colored her voice as she faced him.

"Then you know his bloodlines are crucial to producing the perfect Nuee saddlebred?"

"Of course." Her tone said it was self-evident. "There isn't another horse like Carazzan anywhere in the world."

How well he knew it. "Then you also know he's wasted here."

She went cold inside. "I'd hardly call my breeding program a waste."

He gestured around. "You have facilities fit for a king— or a princess. But you don't have the room to begin to develop a full-scale breeding program here. At my ranch—"

"You want him, don't you?" She had recognized that he had a hidden agenda from the moment he set eyes on the horse. She just hadn't wanted to believe it was the reason for his interest in her. For a brief interlude she had allowed herself to believe he was serious about offering her an equal partnership in the ranch and an equal chance to pursue her dream. Now she saw his offer for what it was, bait to get from her what he really wanted. Had he kissed her for the same reason?

Her heart caught. She had found pleasure in his kiss and thought he shared her feeling. She had even allowed herself to wonder what else they might share, the desire growing stronger when she found out he was as committed to riding therapy as she was. Now the dream shattered into small bits around her.

She might have known he wanted something from her. In her experience most people wanted something from her. It went with her job. Why should Hugh be any different? Knowing this didn't stop her from feeling a disappointment that ate all the way to her soul.

"I won't pretend I don't want Carazzan, Your Highness," he said, confirming her suspicion. "We both know his particular cross is unparalleled in the world. In the right hands Carrazan will be the most positive influence on the Nuee saddlebred in its history."

"The right hands being yours, I gather," she said, amazed that she could talk around teeth so tightly clenched they hurt. "You're an extraordinary man, Mr. Jordan. I suppose it hasn't occurred to you that I might have plans of my own for Carazzan."

He inclined his head slightly. "I'm sure of it, but I also know Prince Michel doesn't approve of your plans."

"While he does yours."

"Look, I understand how hard this is for you."

"You have no idea how hard it is. It was bad enough growing up in the shadow of two headstrong brothers who both knew what was best for me. But I won't tolerate an outsider snatching my land from my grasp, then expecting me to help him fulfill a dream that is rightfully mine."

"I told you, I'm happy to discuss some kind of partner-ship."

"Where you run the show and I sit back and applaud. I don't think so."

"I'm not your brothers, Your Highness. I would never expect you to take a back seat to me."

"And if we disagreed on some aspect of the breeding program?"

"Somebody has to be the boss."

They both knew who it would be. "No, thanks, Hugh. I may not have the land, but I still have Carazzan." She swung on him, her eyes blazing. "If he means so much to you, why didn't you snatch him from under my nose at the auction?"

"Don't you think I would have if it had been possible?"

"All things are possible if we want them enough."

"It hasn't gained you a ranch."

"Yet."

He spread his hands wide, trying to be reasonable. "Nuee is all hills, valleys, rainforest and coastal dunes. We both know there isn't another piece of land on the whole island capable of setting up the kind of facility Carazzan deserves."

He had done his homework well, she thought grudgingly. The worst of it was, he was right. Michel had known it, too. As long as Hugh owned the land, there was no way for Adrienne to set up a rival facility, at least on Nuee. "Carramer has many islands," she said.

"They're either too populated, the terrain is unsuitable or there's insufficient fresh water," Hugh said, thankful that he had done his homework before buying the land. The curse of it was he understood how the princess felt. He had suffered every bit as much on learning that his ex-wife's scheming had made sure Carazzan had been sold to someone else before he could do anything about it.

When she pulled her stunt, he'd been scouting the South Pacific for the right place to establish the new operation. His intention had been to make the auction his last stop before flying home; that was when he discovered the money missing from his account. With no choice but to return to the states and confront Jemima, he'd lost the chance to secure the horse of his dreams.

He had barely managed to get back on his feet financially when the Nuee land became available. When he learned that Carazzan was also here, he'd decided that fate was offering him a second chance. One blue-blooded woman had snatched his dream from him before. He wasn't about to let another spoiled, pedigreed creature do it again because it amused her.

"Then you won't discuss an outright sale, no matter what I'm prepared to offer." It wasn't a question. Her set expression was answer enough.

She shook her head, and her hair swirled around her in a dark curtain. In spite of his annoyance, Hugh was sorely tempted to thread his fingers through the lustrous mass. He wanted to do much more, if he was honest with himself, but remembering who and what she was kept his hand at his side.

"You could always walk away," she said softly.

"Would you?"

Her eyes blazed, rejecting the idea.

"You don't leave many options to resolve this." Could he be content with using Carazzan's services as a stud horse, assuming the princess would consider it? He knew the answer almost as soon as he thought of the question. It wouldn't satisfy either of them.

Her gesture indicated ownership of the prize. "It is already resolved."

His anger and frustration reached flashpoint. "I should have known someone who would deny her birthright by taking stupid risks with her own safety would also be ready to keep a horse like Carazzan from *his* birthright."

She drew herself up. "I wondered when you'd play that card."

What was she talking about? "What card?"

"Using what you know about me to get what you want."

"It had never occurred to me."

"Then why bring it up now?"

"To convince you to see reason and sell me the horse I need. If you didn't recklessly disregard your family's concerns and your safety for a few cheap thrills, you wouldn't have any secret to worry about."

Bitterness filled her. "You don't know the first thing about why I do it."

He couldn't keep the distaste out of his voice. "No, I don't. Until I was fourteen, no one cared enough about me to worry what I did or where I went. You don't appreciate how lucky you are, princess. You knew where you belonged from the moment you were born. I'll never know who my father was, or why my mother walked out soon after I was born, leaving me screaming my head off on an unmade bed in a rooming house. The police who tried unsuccessfully to trace her knew only that she was young and broke, so she probably couldn't cope with a baby. But when you're that baby, all you know is rejection and abandonment."

It was the longest speech he had ever made about himself to anyone, and he let out an explosive breath. "So don't look for sympathy from me. You can trace your family back centuries, you have brothers who obviously care what happens to you, and all you can do is turn your back on them.''

''Going out in disguise is hardly turning my back on my family.''

He heard an immense weariness in her tone. ''Maybe that's a little extreme,'' he conceded. ''But you have to agree, what you did was hardly responsible behavior.''

''Do you know how tired I get of being responsible?'' She lifted her slight shoulders in an expressive movement. ''Sure, I've always known who I am. I'm not allowed to forget it for a minute. I was reviewing parades and taking salutes when I was seven. Most kids fall asleep during military parades. If I did, it was front-page news.''

He spread his hands wide. ''All right, being royal isn't all beer and skittles. I never thought it was. But what about the people who care about you? How would they have felt if that drunken cowboy had managed to drag you away?''

His shot had hit home, he saw when her eyes clouded. ''They would have been shattered,'' she admitted in a low voice. ''When our parents were killed during a cyclone, I thought my brothers would never smile or laugh again.''

''Yet you'd risk putting them through it again on your account?''

''My staff knew where I was. It was broad daylight, so I felt safe enough.''

''It didn't stop you from getting attacked.''

''No.''

''I want you to promise me you'll never do it again.''

Her eyebrows flew upward. ''Or you'll do what?'' She tensed in sudden understanding. ''You intend to tell Michel when you see him, is that it?''

''If you agree to do the right thing, I won't have to.''

''The right thing being to sell Carazzan to you, I suppose?''

"One has nothing to do with the other. I don't stoop to blackmail, princess."

But he could if he wanted to. She was caught on the horns of the worst dilemma she'd ever faced. She couldn't give up Carazzan, and yet the thought of never being able to escape her royal role again was unthinkable.

"Yield to logic, princess," he went on in a voice he might have used to calm a skittish horse. "I have the land, you have the means to make this stud legendary throughout the riding world. A partnership between us is the only thing that makes sense."

"Not the only thing," she said as an idea began to take shape in her mind. As her thoughts raced she wondered if she was insane. She already owned Carazzan. There was no way Hugh could take him away from her without her consent. But he could take much more from her if he revealed her secret to her brother. "There is another solution."

He regarded her warily. "What do you have in mind?"

"A contest between us."

He looked intrigued. "What kind of contest?"

"A riding event—any equine discipline you nominate."

"With you on Carazzan, I suppose?"

She hesitated. She had planned to ride the stallion. "I can choose another horse."

"Count on it." His certainty sent thrills skittering along her spine, at odds with her feeling of annoyance at being so easily caught out. "Using your home ground and your horses, any contest is bound to be biased enough without loading the dice to that extent."

She tossed her head feeling more alive than she had in a long time. "Afraid to accept a challenge, Hugh?"

Another growl started in his throat. "I've never backed

off from a challenge in my life. But it has to be something new to both of us, so we start even.''

"There is one challenge I've always wanted to tackle,'' she said, feeling a mixture of fear and excitement well up. "The Nuee Trail.''

"The endurance ride up the side of Mount Mayat? Are you crazy? That's one of the toughest trails in the southern hemisphere.''

"Probably,'' she agreed, laughter in her voice. It would certainly be a worthwhile contest. "If I win, the prize is your silence about my…extracurricular activities.''

His eyes narrowed to slits. "And if you lose?''

"I agree to stay in my palace like a good little princess forever more.'' The prospect terrified her, but it would be a spur to winning in itself.

He shook his head. "For the challenge you're proposing, the stakes need to be a lot higher.''

Her alarmed gaze followed his to the beautiful horse, his aristocratic muzzle close enough for his hot breath to fan her neck. Instinctively she placed a hand on the horse's long neck. "Oh no, I won't risk Carazzan.''

"Not even for that land you want so badly?''

She felt her eyes widen. "You're willing to wager the land itself?''

"One way or another, Carazzan belongs there. The winner gets both. The only question is, do you have the courage of your convictions?''

Chapter Four

Each passing second was marked by a heartbeat so loud she wondered if he could hear them. Could she really risk ownership of Carazzan on a ride that would stretch even her horsemanship to the limit? Riding the Nuee Trail had been a rite of passage for young Carramer men for centuries. Women had been permitted to attempt it for only sixty years. Five years ago the trail was included in an international circuit of endurance events and was now recognized as one of the most grueling in the world.

Although she had long dreamed of making the ride, she had only suggested it as a desperate measure, to keep Hugh from reporting her activities to Michel. The stakes he proposed were in another league altogether.

In no hurry for an answer, Hugh's expression taunted her. "You can always promise not to go out incognito again, then we'd have no need of a wager at all."

"How do you know I would keep the promise?"

"I don't, but I suspect your word means a lot to you."

She sighed in frustration. He was right. She could only

act as she did because her brothers had not expressly forbidden it. The trail ride was in the same gray area. "When
the Nuee Trail became part of the world endurance circuit,
I talked to Lorne about competing," she said slowly. "Both
he and Michel rode the trail when they were teenagers."

"But they don't think it's proper for you to compete,"
Hugh guessed.

She nodded. "Not so long ago women were forbidden
to set foot on the mountain at all. Nothing much has
changed."

"Especially for a princess," he finished the thought for
her.

"So much of what other people take for granted is off-
limits to a princess. I have to watch what I say, what I do,
where I go—"

"Whom you love?"

He wasn't sure why he'd said it, but the bleakness
sweeping over her lovely features was a confirmation. He
moved closer and without conscious intention, found her in
his arms.

It was an impulse, her look of vulnerability arousing the
protective instinct that had driven men since they lived in
caves, he told himself. But he felt something more, a need
to take as well as give, to relish as well as ravish.

Under his mouth her lips felt warm and soft and tasted
like honey. The spicy scent he'd first noticed at the ball
clung to her hair and skin, making his head swim. His mind
floated. He forgot that she was a princess and they were in
a stable, neither fact making this the least bit appropriate.

Time hung suspended. He was surprised by the strength
in the slender arms she wrapped around his back and the
sudden awakening of a libido he'd buried in work, in riding, in anything rather than admit it was there.

Now he had no choice. The heaven-sent body pressing

against him mocked his self-imposed celibacy. Breathing like a runner nearing the end of a marathon, he threaded his fingers through the glorious black silk of her hair, then on another impulse lifted the heavy fall and ravished her nape with his teeth.

The pleasure-pain of the love bite made Adrienne gasp. No one had ever done such a thing to her before, so she was unprepared for the flurry of signals and needs that raced through her in response. Letting him kiss her was a mistake, but she could think of no way to undo it, no way to make herself want to.

Carramer was well-known for breeding magnificent males, but they paled beside the man holding her in thrall with his demanding mouth and clever hands. From the moment she set eyes on him she had sensed that Hugh could hold power over her. But her wildest fantasies hadn't prepared her for surrender on this scale. Her position meant she wanted for almost nothing, except a soul mate to merge with, to drown in, which she felt herself at risk of doing now.

What on earth was she thinking? Hugh could never be her soul mate. In slight panic, she pulled away. He released her instantly and took a half step back to give her the space to collect herself. He looked much more composed than she felt until she noticed a slight tightening around his eyes, and the fast beating of a pulse at his throat. It was small consolation that she hadn't been the only one drowning here.

"There's no need to apologize," she said, the tremor she heard in her voice far too betraying.

Amusement danced in his gaze. "I wasn't planning to. As far as I know it isn't a crime to kiss royalty in Carramer, especially when it's by invitation."

She tried to shut her mind to the clamor of needs lodged

there by his kiss. This couldn't be allowed to go any further. "You're imagining things."

"Guilty as charged," he agreed without the slightest trace of remorse. "I wasn't the only one. Your imagination was working overtime, as well, my beautiful princess." His brilliant gaze lanced through her, reading her like a book.

Her anger flared, a close cousin to frustration. In his arms she *had* imagined all sorts of possibilities, most revolving around the drifts of sweet-smelling hay at their feet, inviting them to sink down and take the exploration so much further. Knowing it was impossible left her aching with disappointment.

She was appalled at herself. How could she feel this way about someone she had good reason to dislike? His willingness to use what he knew about her to get what he wanted was bad enough. His pursuit of Carazzan was intolerable. So why did her heart yearn so for his touch? She concealed her rioting emotions beneath a regal coolness. "I didn't mean that kind of imagining."

He raked her with that look of knowing her too well. "Yes, you did."

How did he manage it? She had always been able to mask her true feelings. The art had been instilled in her since childhood. Then Hugh came along and suddenly her emotions were on public display, at least to him. Unnerving to say the least.

She tried for a diversion. "You could be mistaking curiosity for something more."

"Are you telling me you've led such a sheltered life that a man's kisses are still a novelty?"

Her life hadn't been *that* sheltered, as he must have known from her responses. "Hardly. But I also know that a kiss doesn't have to mean anything more than momentary gratification."

He was displeased, she saw by his deepening frown. Had he wanted the kiss to mean more to her? Perhaps he couldn't read her as well as he thought. She felt an odd quirk of satisfaction that he wasn't having everything his own way.

Carazzan nuzzled her shoulder, and she turned away, grateful for the distraction. "It's probably as well to have our curiosity satisfied before we become competitors."

She had spoken without thinking, still not sure that the contest was a good idea, especially after the last few minutes. But she had to do something to get him out of her life...out of her mind...and she couldn't think of a better solution.

"Are you sure you want to go through with the wager?"

She wasn't sure about anything where he was concerned, but she inclined her head. "My horse and my secret against your land. Winner take all."

He shook her offered hand. "Agreed."

Another tremor raced along her fingers, all the way up her arm and down her spine. It came to her that competing with him wasn't nearly as appealing as kissing him, but it was probably a lot safer.

He became all business, making her wonder if the kiss wasn't part of some devious strategy. If she wouldn't sell him Carazzan, the next best thing would be to win him from her. Had she fallen into a carefully set trap? "Did you have something like this in mind all along?" she asked, unable to keep suspicion out of her voice.

The hard planes of his face betrayed nothing. "You were the one who suggested riding the Nuee Trail."

She wasn't fooled by his air of innocence. "You don't seem like a man who acts without thinking things through. You came here for Carazzan. Letting me believe a contest was my idea would be a brilliant strategy."

"If it was a strategy."

His reply told her nothing. "Well it's bound to fail. I don't intend to lose. Not my freedom and not Carazzan."

Fascinated, he watched determination firm her chin and fire her sensational eyes with light. She was wrong about the contest. Until she suggested it, he hadn't thought beyond offering her a partnership as a way to secure Carazzan for his new ranch. But the more he thought about pitting his skills against hers, the more stimulated he became.

He pictured her riding at his side, neck and neck as they fought the difficult terrain for ownership of the mountain. Although she had never tackled that particular trail before, she was on home ground and her horsemanship had made enough headlines for him to know she wouldn't make it easy for him. On his side he had the strength and brute cunning of his upbringing, and a drive to win that she couldn't begin to understand. As far as he could tell, they were well matched.

More of a hazard than the mountain was her effect on him. Like Samson with Delilah, Hugh would need to watch that Adrienne didn't undermine him with her beauty and the simmering passion he'd tasted when he'd kissed her. Maybe she knew how she affected him. He suspected she didn't. But she was quick. It wouldn't take her long to work out that her seductive appeal made a potent weapon.

More men in history had been brought low by seduction than by swords, he thought wryly. With so much at stake, he didn't intend to be among them.

"It should be an interesting contest," he said as much for his own benefit as for hers. "Because I don't plan on losing, either."

She ignored this, but found it less easy to ignore the pounding of her heart. It was hard to believe she was really going through with this. What if she lost Carazzan? She set her shoulders and lifted her head, dismissing losing as an option. "Then we should settle the timing," she said, running her schedule through her mind.

His frown suggested he was doing the same. "I have meetings with agricultural officials here this week, then next week I go to Isle des Anges to meet with Prince Michel." Before acquiring the land, Hugh had studied the government of Carramer and knew that the whole country was ruled by Prince Lorne from the capital, Solano, on the main island of Celeste, while Michel had his seat of government on Isle des Anges, the larger of the two islands he governed.

It was a good arrangement, giving each prince their own domain, Hugh thought. Was that why Princess Adrienne preferred to live on the smallest island, Nuee? Both of her brothers were married and had children, so Adrienne was a long way from the throne. She was also the youngest and female, so he could understand why she would value her independence. He had no brothers or sisters to compete with him, but Hugh still liked his own land under his feet and the feeling of being his own boss.

"You don't spend much time on the other islands, do you?" he asked.

She shook her head. "Only when my official duties require it. The royal residence where the ball was held was built for my grandmother. I always loved visiting her there. When I came of age, it was the obvious choice for my home. This place belonged to her, too, although I've made many changes since I inherited it."

Changes for the better, he thought, looking around appreciatively. The stables were a model of modern design and efficiency. He'd bet they weren't here in her grandmother's day.

He voiced what, to him, was an obvious question. "Michel must have his hands full governing both islands. Why don't they make you the governor of this one?"

Her smile was unexpected and dazzling. Something cramped inside him, as if he'd been kicked in the stomach. "They know better."

He had expected bitterness, maybe a suggestion that she'd tried for the job and been turned down. "Excuse me?"

Her silvery laugh added to his sensation of being king-hit. "Bureaucracy isn't for me. I have enough trouble keeping up with my paperwork as it is, without trying to run a country."

"Unless the paperwork involves your horses," he guessed.

"It doesn't qualify as paperwork. It's a labor of love."

He lowered his head. "It's hardly what I expected to hear, princess. I thought running a country would be part of your education."

"Oh, it was. It just didn't take."

"But running a horse breeding operation did."

"Evidently." Absently she ran a hand down Carazzan's muzzle. The horse nuzzled into her palm, and Hugh felt his throat go dry. Some horses had all the luck.

He made himself swallow. "From the look of things you've done a great job here."

She accepted the compliment with a graceful tilt of her head. "Thank you. I intend to go on doing it."

Her meaning was clear. She planned to win the contest so she could expand her breeding program with Hugh safely out of her hair. Too bad he had the same plan.

He did some quick calculations. "From the sound of things, the contest will have to take place at the end of this week."

So soon? She knew he was right but had to struggle

against a feeling of panic. She told herself the difficulty of the ride was the problem, but knew it had as much to do with the man who would accompany her.

His kiss lingered on her lips like a brand, and she would probably carry the mark of his love bite for several days. The effect would last a lot longer, she suspected, her mind awash with a bewildering mix of wishes and regrets.

She had felt regret for a normal life often enough for it to be an old friend. The wishes were also familiar: someone to love and care for her as she cared for him, a family of her own, a purpose beyond mere ornament. Hugh wasn't the man to give her those things, but he intruded on them, anyway, making her wonder.

She pushed the foolish thoughts away. "I'll need to re-arrange my schedule, organize my staff."

He held up a hand. "No staff. This is strictly between you and me."

"But I'll need to take a bodyguard along, at least."

"You didn't need one at the fair."

"As you keep reminding me, it was a reckless thing to do." Like going out alone with him.

"I'll be there to protect you."

And who would protect her from him? "You can hardly protect me if I'm several miles ahead of you on the trail."

A smile turned up the corners of his so-kissable mouth. "In your dreams."

She suspected that was exactly where he would be, if she wasn't careful. "The trail starts beyond the limits of my property. It would cause comment if I'm seen with a stranger, unaccompanied." Word could even get back to her brothers.

She saw him reach the same conclusion. "Not if Dee is the one riding with me."

She couldn't keep her surprise to herself. "You're actually suggesting I make the ride in disguise?"

"You started it."

"I thought you didn't approve."

"I don't, but to do anything else will invite too much comment. We're at an impasse."

"So you recommend the lesser of two evils?"

His gaze rested thoughtfully on her. "I wouldn't call the option evil, exactly. There are worse fates than riding into a rain forest with a beautiful woman, even if she isn't a princess."

A dreamy sensation took hold of her until she brought herself back to earth. "No matter how I appear to others, inside I am always a princess, Hugh."

Was that some kind of warning? It was probably timely. He already needed to keep reminding himself who she was. Alone in the forest with her, it would be too easy to forget, and he couldn't afford to let himself.

Wasn't one marriage to a princess enough to last him a lifetime? Jemima might not have been royal by birth, but she had been her family's princess, wealthy and spoiled, used to being indulged at every turn. It would be a mistake to let himself fall in love with another of her kind, as he'd just been reminded. He hardened his heart. "I'm not likely to forget who you are, Your Highness."

"The reminder wasn't only aimed at you," she said, and he could swear he heard hurt in her voice. "Even when I go about in disguise, I can't forget my place. As a child I was frequently reminded that my actions reflect on the entire royal family. We govern in trust for our people, and Carramer's stability and prosperity depend on how well we uphold that trust."

Her musical voice faltered a little, as if she had been lectured on the subject more times than she cared for. Hugh felt the higher ground shift underneath him. He wanted to be angry with her for not appreciating what she had, to reject her for who and what she was, but he was starting to suspect that being royal was a mixed blessing. "This ride hardly seems to fit the bill," he pointed out.

"Perhaps not for Princess Adrienne."

But okay for Dee as long as she isn't found out, he read between the lines. A weight of responsibility prompted him to say, "Should we be discussing this at all if your brothers forbade you to do it? Prince Michel didn't strike me as a man who takes kindly to being crossed."

It was a characteristic they shared, Hugh had thought at his first meeting with the prince when he'd been the guest of honor at a business dinner in the States. As well as triggering Hugh's interest in Carramer, the prince had spoken affectionately of his family. With no relatives of his own, Hugh would hate to cause trouble between the princess and her brothers.

Hugh's concern made Adrienne feel like a fool. For a moment she'd thought he was worried on her account. How could she forget that he depended on Michel's goodwill to get his facility up and running?

"They didn't want me to take part in the official endurance race, but that won't take place for months yet. I wasn't forbidden to ride the trail at any other time. So you needn't worry about my actions reflecting on your business activities."

His eyes blazed his fury at her. "Have you considered that I might be concerned on your account?"

She rolled her eyes. "I'll try to remember."

"Do that, princess, because I'm not one of your brothers. When we're out on that trail, there won't be any titles between us. We'll be two riders competing for high stakes.

You may outrank me here, but out there I won't give you any quarter.''

"And I won't ask for any."

"Good."

The air crackled between them. Adrienne could practically feel his anger radiating toward her. Could she be mistaken about the reason for his concern? His look of surprise when she mentioned Michel's goodwill had seemed genuine. "I'm sorry if I misread your concern on my behalf," she said stiffly.

His expression mellowed, and something twisted inside her in response. "You did. I haven't had much practice at playing happy families, and I didn't want to cause friction between you and your brothers.''

She looked thoughtful, digesting this. "Lorne didn't actually forbid me to ride the trail," she admitted. Hugh could swear he saw a glimmer of mischief in her lovely eyes. "His precise words were, 'It isn't appropriate.'''

Hugh had spoken with Michel but had only heard Adrienne's older brother's voice on television, but he didn't doubt that her imitation of the monarch was wickedly accurate. "You realize you're splitting hairs?"

"Splitting heirs, don't you mean? Haven't you ever wanted to do something that everyone around you considered inappropriate?''

He nodded. "Most of what I've done in my life fits that description.'' Especially his marriage, he thought. Now there was a venture into a different world. It was as wildly inappropriate as, say, Princess Adrienne marrying someone like him.

The thought should have amused him, but the tightening sensation he felt in his chest was anything but amusing. Easy boy, he warned himself. This filly's not for you. Heck, she isn't even broken yet. Better leave her to some blue-blooded aristocrat who was used to handling her kind to come along and rein her in. Odd how uncomfortable *that* notion felt.

"Then you should understand why I need to break the mold occasionally."

The worst of it was that he did. He nodded. "We've settled where. As for when, I propose we set off on Friday at first light."

She thought quickly. She could reschedule or delegate her commitments for that day. Pity she couldn't delegate her nerves, as well. "Friday is acceptable to me."

"From what I've read, the trail takes about twelve hours round trip."

"That's in good conditions."

"In bad?"

"Some riders never make it back."

This time the catch in his chest was at the thought of the princess out in the wilderness injured or lost. He tried to pin the feeling on a sense of responsibility for her but suspected it was far more personal.

Remember what's at stake, he ordered himself. Not only the horse to make it legendary but the land to build his dream ranch. Worrying about what might happen to the princess was a good way to forfeit the lot.

"Have you thought about a cover story?"

She smiled. "I don't need one. Michel wanted me to meet you and share my experience with you. I'm doing it."

"I doubt that he had the Nuee Trail in mind as a venue."

"He didn't specify." Michel would probably have a fit if he knew his beloved younger sister was planning to spend twelve hours alone in the rainforest with Hugh, although the prospect sent the blood singing through her veins. She told herself it was because of the high stakes, but knew it wasn't the whole story.

"You'd better spend Thursday night here," she heard herself say, then could have bitten her tongue off. Having him under her roof had been no part of her plan until the words popped out.

"Won't that be 'inappropriate'?"

Probably, but withdrawing the invitation would prove she was well aware of it. "Not with a dozen bedrooms and a full complement of staff. Michel will probably be delighted."

He wouldn't if he knew the thoughts that Adrienne's suggestion had sent flying through Hugh's head. Talk about inappropriate! He made himself focus on Carazzan and the reason he was getting involved with the princess even to this degree.

Tired of being ignored, the horse had begun to push against his mistress's shoulder. His last shove sent her reeling against Hugh. He caught her reflexively and felt her quiver of response as his arms closed around her. He had only meant to steady her, but the moment stretched out. So soon after kissing her, he wanted to taste her mouth again so badly that he ached inside.

But this was Carramer, and she was royal. He did the chivalrous thing and set her carefully back on her feet.

"I'd better stay at the hotel until Friday," he said, knowing he sounded as shaky as a rodeo cowboy after a tough ride.

What just happened here? Adrienne asked herself, hearing her own shakiness reflected in his voice. What the heck just happened? Carazzan had shoved her, and Hugh had caught her. It was no reason to quake inside from head to toe. It didn't bode well for being alone with him for a whole day.

She had better make herself focus on what was at stake.

Her beloved horse, her freedom. What more did she need to keep her mind on her task?

She needed a man, she admitted to herself with a frisson of shock. Having two brothers wanting to run her life should have warned her off the breed for good, but it didn't seem to be working where Hugh was concerned.

She prided herself on being tough, independent, needing no one. Hugh's touch made her wonder how honest she was being with herself.

Suddenly independence began to look a lot like loneliness. In Hugh's arms, feeling his mouth hungrily consuming hers, she'd become aware of a whole range of new needs. Or maybe they weren't new, but age-old ones she'd buried under other activities.

Like the need to be loved.

Now wasn't the time, and Hugh wasn't the man to satisfy her need, she told herself sternly. He didn't want her. He wanted control of everything that was important to her. Maybe after she had shown him he was wrong, she could concentrate on other matters. Like socializing more, and not only at charitable affairs where the youngest male was in his sixties.

"How old are you, Hugh?" she asked, surprising herself.

He looked equally startled. "Thirty-one. Care to examine my teeth, since you won't learn much from my bloodlines?"

Had she been studying him as she would a stock horse? "I was curious," she dissembled and hoped he wouldn't ask, "curious about what?"

He didn't but regarded her with a wary intensity that sent ripples of awareness all the way to the soles of her feet. She turned away. "While we're here, you'd better choose a horse for the ride."

"That's your department," he said. "I like something with a bit of spirit."

She shot him a teasing look. "Aren't you afraid that I'll saddle you with a hack that can't find its way out of its own stall?"

"In the first place I doubt you own a horse fitting that description, and in the second, I think you'd prefer to win fair and square."

How well he knew her already. She wasn't sure she liked it. "You're right, I do. But you're wrong about the horses. We have a few gentle old characters that we keep for the children with the most serious disabilities."

He hadn't thought of that. "As long as you don't saddle me with a rocking horse to ride on the trail," he cautioned.

She made a heart-crossing gesture. "You have my word."

"Good enough for me."

A sudden surge of anticipation caught him unawares. He was actually looking forward to the challenge, he realized. To a rider it was the ultimate test, but it was more than that. He liked the idea of being out in the wilderness with the princess.

Not the princess—Dee, he amended the thought. When they set off at dawn on Friday they would be equals, rivals certainly, but equals for the duration. No titles, no pomp and circumstance, just two people out to prove a point.

It didn't escape him that the point could cost him dearly. As he had told the princess, he didn't plan on losing. Not only did the idea offend him, he wasn't about to let Carazzan slip through his fingers a second time.

He looked at the stallion's magnificent head almost resting on the princess's shoulder. It seemed a shame to separate the two of them, but he was going to have to, if the dream Big Dan Jordan had seeded in him was ever to become a reality. For a moment, before Hugh dismissed the thought, he wished there was a way for both of them to win.

Adrienne gave the horse a lingering look as if reluctant to leave. "It's time we returned to the others."

As if on cue, Cindy appeared at the stable door. Her assistant looked flustered, the princess thought. "There you are, Your Highness," she said. "We're waiting for you to join us for afternoon tea."

And the children were probably eyeing the cakes and other goodies with longing, forbidden to touch them until the princess appeared, she thought guiltily. She understood the censure in her assistant's tone. "I'm sorry, Cindy. We got talking about horses, and I lost track of the time. I'll come at once."

Cindy's curious gaze flickered to Hugh, but he kept his expression bland. They *had* been talking about horses—in between exchanging a kiss that had rocked him to his core. He sighed. It was going to be a long time until Friday.

Chapter Five

The first thing Hugh saw when he got out of the car the princess had sent for him was Her Highness exercising Carazzan. His heartbeat quickened. She looked so stunning that it was hard to believe he hadn't conjured her up out of a dream.

Under a pale morning sky stained with the first red-gold rays of the sun, she rode as if she and the horse were one. Carazzan's coat had a sheen of gold and the brisk morning air turned his breath into steaming clouds.

As the princess reined the horse in, Carazzan pranced around and pawed at the ground, expressing his displeasure at being brought to a standstill. The princess leaned forward and patted the arching neck, then looked straight at Hugh.

The sound of the car must have alerted her, or else it was the strange sense of awareness Hugh could feel vibrating between them that drew her gaze to him. She was too far away for him to read her expression but he imagined there was some of the same excitement he felt radiating through her.

Was it at the prospect of a hard ride through new country, or the company he was about to keep? Suddenly he saw the princess urge Carazzan into a dramatic turn, and they galloped toward him.

As the powerhouse combination thundered down on him, Hugh stood his ground. His heart thudded but he stood as if planted. Lord, they were an impressive sight. The princess's dark hair flew out around her riding hat, and her long legs, encased in form-fitting jodhpurs and leather boots, controlled the stallion with a skill that made Hugh's mouth feel dry as he had a sudden, breathtaking vision of himself in the horse's place.

Stop it, he ordered himself angrily. It was bad enough that his attention was on the rider rather than the horse he had come to claim, without letting his imagination run away with him completely. It didn't stop images of himself together with the princess from running riot through his head.

If he was to achieve his goal, he had to keep his mind clear. Easier said than done, he accepted, as horse and rider bore down on him. The princess was not only beautiful, she rode like the wind, expertly controlling the ton of horseflesh beneath her without the slightest trace of fear.

Dust flew from beneath Carazzan's hooves as she reined him to a stop that left Hugh's heart in his mouth. They were no more than an arm's length away from him, and he didn't know who was breathing harder, Carazzan or himself.

His respect for the princess's riding skills notched higher. So did a feeling of physical arousal that was as strong as it was out of place. It slammed into him with a force as great as if the stallion had actually run him down. He recognized the cause. Against all common sense, he wanted Adrienne de Marigny.

Dear heaven, what had he gotten himself into?

Hugh hadn't moved a muscle, Adrienne noticed in unwilling admiration. She knew it was foolhardy to ride Carazzan at him. It was akin to pointing a loaded gun at someone. But she hadn't been able to resist the temptation.

He looked so superbly masculine, standing at the edge of the arena, that she had felt challenged by his presence. The early-morning light had carved his strong features into planes of light and shadow, a primitive statue rather than a man. Then he moved, and she remembered the heat of his body pressed against her and the fire he had kindled in her blood when he kissed her.

She ached for a repeat even as she knew she mustn't allow it to happen. The reason stirred beneath her. Carazzan's restless movements were transmitted through her calves and thighs as ripples of muscular sensation that intensified the yearning she felt.

A soul-deep hunger assailed her until she reined herself in as she had done Carazzan. "Good morning, Hugh," she made herself say evenly as she slid to the ground.

A groom emerged from the shadow of the stables and took the reins from her. She acknowledged him with a distracted nod, and he led Carazzan away. She was usually happy to walk her horse around until cooled down, then groom him herself. Today she had more pressing problems.

Did she imagine it or was Hugh's smile forced as he said, "Good morning, Your Highness. I thought we had enough riding in front of us today without getting a head start."

No doubt he was also counting the cost if he lost today's challenge. *When* he lost it, she added grimly to herself. Aloud she said, "I always exercise Carazzan at first light. I saw no reason to miss it today."

He was probably also jealous, she told herself, feeling

something similar grip her at the sight of Carazzan's reins in the groom's hands. How could she bear to see the magnificent horse being led away for good? She couldn't, wouldn't allow it to happen.

She didn't tell Hugh that she had been too keyed up to snatch more than a few hours of sleep, blaming her restlessness on the challenge ahead. She refused to think it was because she kept reliving his kiss over and over, and touching her fingers to the slight mark his teeth had left at her nape.

"Have you had breakfast?" she asked as he fell into step beside her.

He acknowledged the question with a nod. "At the hotel. You?"

"Enough to satisfy me for now." The reality was more like a cup of coffee and a sweet roll, but she was so edgy that she couldn't contemplate eating anything more substantial before setting off.

"Then we can start right away. We have twelve hours of hard riding ahead of us."

As if she needed reminding. "Our horses should be ready for us by now. Everything we're likely to need will be in our saddlebags."

"Food and drink?" he assumed.

She nodded. "I had packs made up with provisions, first aid kit, a map of the terrain and compass for each of us, that kind of thing."

"You seem to have thought of everything."

Everything but her own feelings, she thought as she matched him stride for stride. His legs were longer, forcing her to stretch to keep up. As she would have to stretch to keep up with him on the trail, she suspected. Her brave claim that she would set the pace seemed foolhardy now as she contemplated what lay ahead of them.

She could always pull out, she told herself. No one else knew of the wager they'd made so it would be Hugh's word against hers if she changed her mind and decided not to risk ownership of Carazzan after all.

She would know, she thought. Every time she rode the horse it would be a reminder of failure. Not only failure to test herself to the limit, but to reach out and grasp her dream. All she had to do was complete the round trip ahead of Hugh, and his land would be forfeited to her. Carazzan would have a home worthy of him, and she would be mistress of a domain her brothers couldn't interfere with.

If she lost, Hugh would be the one creating the dream. A new fear struck her. Why hadn't it occurred to her before now that if he won, she would have to endure more than his ownership of Carazzan. She would have to endure his presence on Nuee for good.

This thought, more than any other, almost made her withdraw. It took a sheer effort of will to keep walking.

Two of the splendid horses she had shown Hugh on his previous visit were saddled up and waiting, loosely tied to railings near the main stables. She gestured to a frisky chestnut mare. "I'll be on Gypsy. This is Avatar, your mount." She reached up to caress the muzzle of a tall black beauty. Her smile mocked him. "I guarantee he's no rocking horse."

Hugh could see that for himself. To his expert eye, the black gelding looked fiery and responsive. A thrill of anticipation coursed through him. For a moment he'd suspected that the princess wanted to back out, but now it was obvious that she was as determined as he was to see this through.

He was dressed for serious riding in a cream-colored long-sleeved shirt, jodhpurs and lace-up leather boots, with an Australian Drizabone jacket in case the weather changed. He'd purchased a narrow-brimmed Carramer cowboy hat downtown and now he jammed it on to his head. "Ready when you are, Dee."

His use of her alias brought her head up, and she remembered his warning. No titles and no quarter given.

He reached for the gelding. "What are we waiting for?"

She went still. "Dee isn't with us yet," she said quietly.

He could have kicked himself. He'd been so dazzled by her appearance on Carazzan that he had forgotten she couldn't just saddle up and ride off, as he could. The reminder of their differences was timely. He nodded. "I'll wait here for you."

Princesses were evidently more punctual than wives because Adrienne—Dee—was back in under ten minutes. The transformation startled him. She had tied her lustrous black hair into a knot at her nape and replaced her custom-fit riding hat with a traditional narrow-brimmed Carramer cowboy's hat. It did a lot more for her than it did for him, he thought. Huge sunglasses concealed much of her aristocratic features.

All the same he knew he would have recognized her anywhere. "You look great, Dee," he said around the sudden tightening in his gut. They were going to be alone in the wilderness all day. He had better get used to thinking of her as a rival, rather than a woman he would rather be alone with in a more intimate location.

She inclined her head, the regal gesture arguing with her plain appearance. "I'm glad to see you brought a coat. The weather on Mount Mayat can change in a minute."

He nodded, indicating the oilcloth coat he'd added to his pack. "I checked the forecast. We might get some rain, but otherwise it looks good."

She grimaced. "Rain in Carramer means something

other than the rain you're probably accustomed to. Ours is generally the monsoonal kind.''

"Chickening out, princess?" he asked in a teasing voice.

She felt her jaw harden. "Just issuing fair warning. And it's supposed to be Dee for the duration."

He nodded coolly, but alarm surged through him. Dee or not, he was going to have a hard time keeping his mind where it belonged today. The way she swung her lithe body onto the mare made his mouth go dry. The long legs settling either side of the horse's withers was another test of his restraint.

"Chickening out?" Adrienne called down to him as she saw him hesitate.

He came out of the trance he was in and mounted Avatar. He led the gelding into a comfortable walk, getting used to the horse, she noticed approvingly. As she walked back after transforming herself into Dee, she had seen him introduce himself to the horse and offer an apple from his pocket. Now they circled the arena like old friends.

She had kept her word and given him a first-class horse. Avatar liked cantering, jumping logs and riding in steep country. Her own horse, Gypsy, was Avatar's sister, and the two got along famously well. Not like her and Hugh, she thought. When this day was over, one of them would effectively be out of the breeding business for good.

It wasn't going to be her, she promised herself, although thinking of Hugh leaving Carramer wasn't as satisfying as she thought it should be. If he lost the land, there would be nothing to keep him here. Certainly not her. And he wouldn't want to watch from the sidelines while she built the dream that should have been his. All the same, the more she thought about what it would cost him, the less sweet the victory seemed.

Keep thinking like that and you're certain to lose, she

told herself. Unlike Hugh she didn't have the option of leaving, so she had better make sure she won. Urging Gypsy into a walk, she aimed the horse toward the hills. Hugh was close behind her. This was traditional riding country so no one paid them any attention as she led the way along a quiet road that bounded her property on one side toward the nearby foothills. Strictly speaking, the trail—and, therefore, the contest—didn't start until much higher up. It started in forest so dense that if more than two riders set off together, the first horse was concealed from the last.

The approach to the trail followed one of the original bridle tracks blazed through the forest by the first ranchers to bring cattle into the area in 1840, followed by jade miners in the 1860s. Moving at a comfortable pace, Adrienne was pleased when she spotted a rare Firebird, Carramer's national bird, with its wide wingspan and distinctive flame-colored crest. She took it as an omen.

"From here we climb the Staircase Spur until we reach the start of the trail," she told Hugh when they stopped to consult their maps. Around them the rainforest floor was filled with three-meter high ferns and towering stands of mountain ash.

He stabbed a finger at his own map. "Then it's straight up here through Devil's Pass and Rocky Plain to the summit where the first to arrive collects the marker kept there and brings it back down," he supplied, his eyes dancing. "First to bring it back down is the winner."

She regarded him in surprise. "You've done your homework."

He pushed his hat back on his head. "First rule of survival in business—know your enemy."

"Am I your enemy?"

"We are rivals."

"But only for a horse and land. Surely there are more important things in life?"

His mouth snapped into an unforgiving line. "In my country's history, sometimes having a horse and land made the difference between living and dying."

"But not now."

"Maybe not in the literal sense. You were born to this country, so you'll never know how it feels not to belong anywhere, without even a name of your own."

"Where does Hugh Jordan come from, then?"

His expression softened slightly and she felt an answering jolt. "Big Dan Jordan was the last of my foster fathers. I took his name out of respect for him and his memory."

"Your last foster father?"

"I had four. The first three sent me back to the boys' home. They said I was too much trouble."

"And were you?"

He nodded. "Since I had no family of my own, I didn't want to play, 'let's pretend' with theirs. I know there are good people out there fostering kids like me, and I have the greatest respect for them, but the ones I got didn't want to acknowledge who and what I was. They tried to get me to forget my history and blend in. I guess they didn't want to be reminded that I wasn't their own child, so I made it my business to remind them."

"I take it Big Dan Jordan wasn't like that?"

"He urged me to value my history because it meant I could be whoever and whatever I wanted."

Unlike me, she thought. Aloud she said, "He sounds like a good man."

"The best."

"And the name 'Hugh'?"

He cleared gravel from his throat. "That came from the nurse who took care of me after I was found. I gather I wasn't the prettiest or healthiest baby, but then babies of drug-addicted mothers seldom are. It was a long time before I could be considered for fostering.''

He wouldn't welcome pity, she sensed, but her heart constricted at the thought of a tiny baby being abandoned in that condition. It was obvious he didn't blame the young, troubled woman who had given him birth and then left him when she couldn't cope with a child on top of her own problems. "Don't you wonder about your parents?" she asked, unable to imagine being so adrift from her own past.

"Of course. But I refuse to build fantasies about a couple of lost souls, seeking comfort where they could.''

"Not even when you were the result?''

He shrugged. "Without the kind of start I had, I might never have gotten where I am now.''

It was an unusually generous attitude, she couldn't help thinking, as her admiration for him grew once more. If he kept this up, she might be tempted to do something rash, like let him reach the summit first. If the price hadn't been so high... She dismissed the notion with an effort. She had agreed to play fair, and that meant doing everything in her power to win. A man like Hugh wouldn't accept victory on any other terms.

As if to confirm her thought, he said, "Are we going to sit here jawing all day? At this rate I'll never beat you to the summit and back.''

She gave him a wide-eyed glare. "News for you, Hugh. That marker already has my name on it.''

"You couldn't fit all those titles.''

"But I could fit 'Dee.' ''

Laughing, she spurred Gypsy into a fast canter. Hugh was right behind her, pushing her to a pace that made the horses' bodies sleek with sweat, hoofs crashing up narrow paths winding between silver-barked mountain ash and the twisted arms of canyon trees.

On the steepest sections, she grabbed handfuls of Gypsy's mane and stood in the stirrups, leaning forward to take the weight off the horse's back. Out of the corner of her eye she saw Hugh doing the same.

After what felt like endless riding but was in reality about three hours, they arrived at a wide button of grassy plain on top of a ridge of the Nuee Divide. On one side rain flowed into tributaries of the Mayat River and on the other to a web of rivers leading to the Pacific Ocean.

A long way below her, the serpentine loops of the Mayat River sliced through range upon range of blue-misted mountains marching toward the horizon. On the edge of the plain she spotted the pennant her staff had set up to mark the halfway point to the summit. They had agreed to stop there for lunch. The first to reach it would also set off first after the break. She was going to do it.

She touched the red flag a bare five minutes before Hugh's horse bore down on it. That meant she would have only a five-minute head start when the contest resumed. It wasn't much of a lead, but it would have to do. And it was better than the alternative.

"You took some almighty risks back at the last river crossing," he said as they ate lunch from their packs. The horses grazed at a slight distance, enjoying the fresh, sweet meadow grass.

She pointed to the pennant. "I'm leading, aren't I?"

"It won't do you much good if you get yourself killed."

"You'd have the horse and land."

"And a price on my head from your brothers." He reached for an apple from his pack. "Why do you take risks like this, Dee?"

She settled her back against the rough bark of a canyon

tree. She could have pointed out that he was taking the same risks. "The glib answer would be 'because it's there,' the same reason why mountaineers climb Everest."

"To push yourself to the limit?"

"That's part of it."

"You said it was the glib answer. What's the real one?"

"To push my boundaries. You said that you loved Big Dan Jordan because he showed you how to invent yourself."

"Is that what you're doing? Reinventing yourself?"

Adrienne rolled the wrapper from her lunch into a tiny ball. "Probably. Like you and your foster families I'm expected to play a role. It sometimes feels like having a part in a soap opera, except that I'm expected to live the part off camera as well as on."

"So occasionally you take the makeup off and see who's underneath."

She hadn't expected to be understood so swiftly. The realization gave her a jolt. "That's it exactly."

"Doesn't mean you have to get yourself killed to prove a point."

After the understanding, his disapproval came as a shock. "Are you saying I should just accept my life as it is?"

"Nobody has to accept what they're given in life, Dan Jordan's first law. If I'd done that, I'd be living on the streets now, probably on a chemical high most of the time."

She leaned forward, clasping her arms around her bent knees, finding it hard to imagine him in such a situation. "What made you change your mind?" She couldn't believe a lecture from anyone, even someone he obviously respected as much as he had his foster father, could make Hugh Jordan do something against his will.

"You don't want to know." For some reason Hugh

didn't want to tell her that it had taken a beating to make him wake up to himself. Afraid to dent her image of him as a take-no-prisoners he-man? Afraid he wouldn't measure up to her high-status brothers who had needed no such lesson as far as he knew?

Jemima had used arguments like those against him. Her brother was a corporate lawyer instead of a prince, but her reasoning had been the same—Hugh might have married an aristocrat, but in no way could he ever measure up to a true thoroughbred.

He had put up with it because Dan Jordan had taught him to respect women, and also because his ex-wife's opinion had stopped mattering to him by the time she resorted to belittling him. The thought made him pause. Did that mean the princess's opinion *did* matter to him?

"I do want to know," she said into the lengthening silence.

He took a deep breath. He couldn't allow what she thought of him to matter. "All right. Dan goaded me until I took him on, then he beat the tar out of me."

She looked as shocked as Hugh had expected, but instead of derision, what he got was, "That's hardly good child psychology. Wasn't there anyone you could complain to, who could protect you?"

She was concerned on his account. The thought stunned Hugh, it was so novel. "He didn't hurt me, just cuffed me around a bit, bear to bear cub," he grunted. "Dan wanted to show me that my fists weren't the answer to everything. When I was as riled as I was that day, I couldn't think straight. I thought I could take on anyone, but Dan made me see that I couldn't. He also reminded me that the next man I challenged might have a knife or a gun."

Her heart turned over. "You could have been killed."

He rubbed the back of his neck as if a painful memory

was lodged there. "Dan's point exactly. I discovered that thinking's better."

"What are you thinking now."

"I'm thinking this is a mistake."

It was the last thing she had expected him to say. "Why?"

"Surely there are other ways to solve this situation."

"You mean you'd rather beat the tar out of me?" She heard how her voice vibrated as she threw his words back at him. She wasn't as bullheaded as Hugh had evidently been as a teenager, so there was no need for such a painful lesson. It was more the thought of being so totally in his power that appalled and excited her in equal measure.

He shook his head. What he was tempted to do wasn't as painful, but it was physical. "I mean we should call this race off and work the problem out like adults."

"I thought we'd tried that."

"Not hard enough."

She jumped to her feet. "In my experience, when my brothers ask me to discuss something reasonably, they usually mean for me to see it their way."

He uncoiled from the moss-covered rock, more annoyed than he should have been by the comparison to her brothers. "This has nothing to do with them. It's between you and me."

"It's always to do with them. They run the country."

"And you?"

"Me, as well, when it suits them."

He moved closer, as if drawn by an invisible connection between them. "Then how come you're living on Nuee instead of Isle des Anges or Celeste?"

She laughed but heard the nervousness in it as he loomed alongside her. Lord, but he was big. "Okay, having my own place was one of my two rebellious acts."

"And Dee?"

"She's the other. I decided long ago that she's an only child, answerable to no one."

"Funny, that's exactly how I used to describe myself."

Her chin came up to hide her consternation at his sudden closeness. "It was true, wasn't it?"

"It's never true. We are all answerable to somebody, even if it's only our own consciences."

"Are you saying I should stop going out as Dee to ease my conscience?"

"What do you think?"

"I think you're trying to undermine my confidence so I lose the challenge."

He loomed over her. "You don't know me very well, do you?"

"I was briefed on your background."

Almost blotting out her sun, he looked dangerous. And attractive. Dangerously attractive.

"Did your briefing include my beliefs, my fears, my fantasies?"

She shook her head, her mouth going dry. "Of course not. Only things like your professional life and your charity concerns." The air felt charged between them. She had to say something to defuse it. "I also know your marriage was a failure."

"You know nothing about my marriage."

"What happened, Hugh?"

"Didn't your files tell you that, too?"

"Only that your ex-wife was an ambassador's daughter. And she was beautiful." Adrienne had seen pictures of the heiress who had been Hugh's wife for two years. She could have been a model.

Bitterness twisted his features. "Beautiful on the outside, maybe."

"What went wrong?"

"I didn't give her everything she wanted."

Adrienne wasn't sure where the revelation came from. "And you think I'm like her?"

"Aren't you?"

The simple question sliced through her like a knife, making her temper flare. "How typically male. You don't have a patent on being misunderstood, Hugh. An accident of birth doesn't automatically make you a noble savage any more than it makes me a poor little rich girl."

"Poor little rich girl?" he echoed her words.

"I said I'm not one," she snapped back. "I appreciate the advantages I've been given, and I certainly don't feel sorry for myself when other people have to contend with much worse. But it doesn't stop me from wanting to make a life for myself outside the mold. Why is it okay for you but not for me? Because you're a man, is that it?"

Before she could stop herself she lashed out. She had never lost control to that extent before, and shock throbbed through her as he caught her hand in midair on the way to his face. "I...I'm sorry," she said barely above a whisper.

He looked down at her with a face like thunder. "Princess or not, I don't take that from anyone."

His fingers felt like iron banded around her wrist. She lifted her face, refusing to be cowed although inwardly was another matter. In the tone of a royal command, she said, "Kindly release me."

His stony expression didn't relax. "I see Her Highness is back. So much for breaking the mold. That's the difference between us, princess. You only do it when it suits you."

He was right, she thought in stunned realization. Why hadn't she seen it before? Dee was a game, a wraith who only came out when it was safe. Whenever the real world threatened, the princess swiftly intervened.

Then she remembered the Nuee Show. "I didn't turn back into a princess at the Nuee Show."

"And now?"

Before she could answer he pressed her back against the smooth bark of a canyon tree. With her arm clamped in his grasp and held high over her head, she felt achingly vulnerable as he pinned her against the tree with the full length of his body.

His mouth was harsh, demanding. It wasn't as much a kiss as an exploration. As if he sought the real Adrienne beneath the layers of royal conditioning. First the princess peeled away beneath his questing mouth. The loving kisses of her family, the duty kisses of her social connections bore no resemblance to the raw power she experienced in Hugh's kiss.

Then Dee surfaced, gulping air as he ravaged her throat and pushed aside the open collar of her shirt to savor the tender valley between her breasts. Her chest heaved. Dee could be his lover, she sensed at some timeless level of hyperawareness. But Dee wasn't real. So who was responding to his kiss with such wanton abandon?

Adrienne.

The thought came to her in a blinding flash. He kissed her as a man kissed a desirable woman, forcing her to respond out of her authentic self. With no yardstick for how to behave simply as Adrienne, she kissed him back and wrapped her free hand around his neck, winding her fingers through his hair as she gave of herself, fully and completely, knowing it was for the very first time.

When he finally lifted his head and let her arm drop to her side, she felt hollow, as if he had scooped out her very center and left her empty. She stared at him, feeling her eyes wide and moist. "What just happened here?"

"I kissed you," he said simply. He looked much more in control than she felt, and it hurt to think he could be indifferent to the emotions boiling through her. She wanted to lash out at him again but, remembering the result the first time, kept her hands rigidly at her sides.

It didn't stop her from hating him for what he had made her feel, as he said coolly, "You kissed me back. You—not Dee, and not the princess."

With an effort she summoned her voice. "How did you know?"

"It wasn't difficult. For all of thirty seconds, you forgot yourself and just gave."

"And you took," she said, unable to hide her bitterness. She hated him for using her to prove a point, when it had meant so much more to her.

"That's the way it usually works."

She gave a derisive laugh. "You see yourself as superior to people like your ex-wife and my brothers and me. But you're no different. You're every bit as arrogant and opinionated in your own way as the people you disdain."

She had struck a nerve, she saw, when he went still. "There is a difference," he said after a long pause, "I took from you, all right. But nothing you didn't give me willingly. And I also gave."

"Gave me what?"

"Satisfaction. And a taste for more of the same."

She felt the color pooling high on her cheeks. "You are unbelievable. I have absolutely no desire to have you kiss me or touch me again."

His gaze settled on her mouth. "None whatsoever?"

She wanted to lick her lips but refused to betray herself to that extent. "None."

"Then you wouldn't want me to take you in my arms again and undo the buttons of that so-prim white shirt, then plunge my hands inside and..."

Desire warred with anger inside her. "Stop this. Of course I wouldn't. I don't need anything from you."

"Then what are we doing out here?"

She was sure he knew she hadn't meant the challenge. She felt shaky, as if she'd already ridden the entire course, and suspicion welled up. "If this *is* some trick to stop me from winning—"

"We both know it isn't," he said. "If it was, I'd be at the summit by now instead of letting myself get sidetracked."

A small surge of elation took her. So he wasn't entirely indifferent to her, after all. Kissing her had been no part of his original plan, any more than her response had formed part of hers. All the same, her response disturbed her. She had thought only of victory. Of beating him to the summit and back and claiming his land and her horse. Now she sensed that it would be a hollow triumph at best.

When had she begun to care about Hugh as a person, she wondered? The suspicion came swiftly—at the moment he had kissed her, not as the princess, or her alter ego, Dee, but as Adrienne. For an instant he had forced her to live in the moment as herself. No one had ever done that for her before.

She was under no illusion that it promised anything more. Hugh's attitude toward his ex-wife warned her there was no place for someone like Adrienne in his life. He hadn't said it in so many words, but she got the impression that he'd escaped that cage once. Not even a princess was going to lure him back in.

Did she want to try? She was better off not considering it. They were born opposites and now rivals. Hugh had come to love Big Dan Jordan for beating the tar out of him, but she didn't think fighting Hugh would work for her. Loving him was even less of an option.

So there was no point in fantasizing about something that couldn't happen. Because in spite of everything, she still intended to win.

Chapter Six

Unbelievably the riding got worse from there. Adrienne
was aware that sometimes Hugh led the way and sometimes
she did, but most of the time she had too much to do keeping herself and the horse in one piece, to worry about keeping score.

Gypsy had her worried, too. Adrienne normally loved to
ride the responsive mare, but today it was all she could do
to keep the horse aimed in the right direction. Was it the
difficulty of the ride, or was the mare picking up Adrienne's
own tension? A little of both, she suspected.

The exhilaration of cantering along the old bridle tracks
was forgotten in the struggle to make any headway on the
treacherous, barely marked path. Above her, 600 feet of
steep cliffs glowed platinum in the afternoon light. Below,
a ravine fell away for a nerve-testing 1500 feet. She tried
not to look down.

The crisp mountain air no longer lifted her spirits as
much as it seared her lungs. Gypsy was mountain bred, but
she still found the going tough. Adrienne started to under-

stand why her brothers hadn't wanted her to do this. It wasn't a trail ride. It was a journey to hell.

The trees opened out onto a narrow belt of snow plain, and she reined Gypsy in, grateful for a chance to rest the laboring horse. If Hugh was behind her, Avatar wouldn't make it to the summit without a breather, either. If he was that far ahead—and she doubted it—she was already in trouble, so there was little harm in taking the respite.

She looked around for her adversary, but the forest was too dense for her to see, and the thick undergrowth blanketed most sounds.

Unfortunately, the silence and aloneness made it hard to avoid thinking. She ran the back of her hand across her mouth. She had no words for what was going on inside her. It was as if Hugh's kiss had triggered an internal meltdown, forcing her to question everything she thought she knew up to this point.

She took a long swallow of spring water from her canteen and felt a few droplets trickle down the cleft between her breasts. Refreshing as it felt, it was also a vivid reminder of where Hugh's lips had traveled.

She must look a sight, she thought, picturing the sweaty tangle of her hair under the borrowed cowboy hat. She'd shed the sunglasses miles before. Who was going to recognize her up here? They had probably left a panda mask of dust and sweat on her face.

Hugh hadn't seemed to care. He had kissed her like a man with nothing but passion on his mind. Thanks to him, it had been the only thing on hers, she thought. What would it be like to be truly, deeply loved by such a man?

She might be innocent in many ways, but it didn't take much to imagine herself in his bed, his muscular body covering hers as they explored the real meaning of passion.

She sensed that he wouldn't rest until he'd taken them both to the stars and back.

The thought was so unsettling that she took another quick swallow of water. He thought of her in the same unflattering light as his ex-wife, so why torture herself? In any case, with no family history and a dubious upbringing, Hugh was the last man she would be permitted to love.

Thinking of her brothers' reaction if they knew, she shook her head. This was one decision she couldn't allow them to make for her, or stop her from making when the time was right. She would do almost anything for her country but that. Whom she married would be between her and the man she loved.

Hugh.

She hadn't conjured him up out of fantasy. He really was crashing into the open on Avatar. He saw her and brought the horse to a stop. Avatar was breathing as heavily as Gypsy, she saw, as both horses snorted steam. She knew how they felt.

She couldn't resist. "I wondered when you'd catch up."

His compelling eyes flamed as he slid out of the saddle and dropped Avatar's reins over his head. "Catch up? I've been ahead of you most of the way."

"Then how come you're behind me now?"

"Avatar lost footing on the last climb. I had to walk him to the top of the slope."

She knew the place he meant. She'd had to do the same. And she was still in front. Elation pumped through her. He needed to rest his horse. She was ready to saddle up again. She was going to win.

She caught Gypsy and hoisted herself into the saddle. "See you at the summit."

"I'll give you a hand to reach the marker when you get there."

A toss of her head answered for her as she urged Gypsy back into the trees.

Hugh's feelings were mixed as he watched her go. He was too competitive to want her to win, and yet he regretted the only alternative. What's happening to you, Jordan, he asked himself? Getting soft in your older days?

She looked very different from the woman he'd rescued at the show, and even further removed from the princess he'd danced with at the palace. Outwardly she looked like any other rider foolish enough to tackle this fiendish trail: dirty, exhausted, fighting for breath in the rarefied air.

She looked beautiful.

When he kissed her, he had felt her touch some hidden well of emotion inside him. He didn't want it, but that didn't stop it from happening. It was there now, clamoring for attention, making him think about her instead of where Avatar was putting his feet.

She was Jemima all over again, he told himself. He'd believed himself in love with her, too, mooning over photographs of them together and eagerly planning their next date. Marriage to her had seemed like heaven until the crunch came.

This felt different somehow. If he had to put a label on it, he would say it felt more real. Not that he hadn't wanted Jemima. If anything, her beauty and unattainability had made her as irresistible as a one-of-a-kind collectible.

Alarm gripped him. He had accused Jemima of marrying him for all the wrong reasons. For the first time it occurred to him that he might also have wanted a trophy wife to prove to himself and the world how far he'd come. Had he ever loved Jemima for herself? To his dismay, he was no longer sure.

Was he attracted to the princess for the same reason? That he could answer. Not a chance. He had felt drawn to her from first meeting, when he only knew her as Dee, the woman with the balloon. Far from adding to the attraction, finding out who she was had complicated everything.

Damn Adrienne for making him question so many things. It was probably part of her strategy to psych him out, to stop him from winning this challenge, he thought. While he was agonizing over a kiss that was best forgotten, she was probably at the summit, snatching the marker that should be his.

The thought spurred him on. He drank liberally, doused water over himself, hat, clothes and all, and mounted Avatar. Before he could aim the horse at the pass leading to the summit, he noticed a buildup of cloud behind him. It was so heavy that it obscured the peaks of the neighboring ranges.

The weather forecast had predicted rain. With a sense of foreboding, he recalled Adrienne's comment about rain on Nuee tending to be monsoonal. He shivered, although the water he'd splashed himself with had started to dry almost as soon as it touched his clothes. This mountain was no place to be in a monsoon.

Had Adrienne seen the ominous buildup? He doubted it. She had seemed completely focused on winning the challenge. He should be, too, but not at the risk of their lives. It was too late to do more than hope it wouldn't come to that.

The storm was still only a threat when he reached the final approach to the summit, now only six hundred feet away. He had closed the lead until Adrienne was only minutes ahead of him. She had jumped off Gypsy by the time he reached her.

He soon saw why. The remaining rocky track was almost vertical.

Obviously getting ready to lead her horse up the rocky

incline, Adrienne gave him a wary look as she stripped down to a sleeveless sweater. It did amazing things for her shape, seriously tempting him to take his mind off the task, until she said, "That marker still has my name on it."

With scant ceremony he ripped off his own shirt and rammed it into his pack. "In your dreams, princess."

"Dee," she snapped. A princess wouldn't be out half-dressed, alone on a mountain with a man, while the weather closed in around them. She wondered if Hugh had noticed.

She noticed more than she wanted to, most of it having nothing to do with the weather. Without his shirt, Hugh's bare biceps gleamed with sweat from his exertion. He was breathing hard but not as hard as she was at the sight of his broad, masculine chest and the way a scattering of dark hairs arrowed downward to disappear below his belt line.

She drew a shuddering breath. He was close enough for her to reach out and touch. If she did, would she feel his heart beating under her hand? The temptation was almost overwhelming.

Tired to the bone, she longed to turn and bury her face against his hard chest and feel his strong arms close around her. The thought shocked her into action.

The summit was waiting, and Hugh was only an arm's length behind her. She made herself recognize his closeness for what it was, a threat to everything she held dear. How could she think of herself in his arms when she should be putting as much distance between them as she could?

Then she had no time to think of anything except keeping her footing on the slippery surface. As her mountain-bred horse jumped boulders, barely breaking stride, Adrienne had to run to keep up.

Suddenly she was on top of Mount Mayat, on a wide swath of grassy snow plain crowning the Nuee Divide. The wild, rugged features of the Mayat Range were all around her, marching toward the horizon.

At the far side of the plain, a cairn of stones held the coveted jade marker that decided who had won this leg of the challenge. She swung herself into the saddle and spurred Gypsy toward it. The thunder of hooves alongside her told her Hugh had kept up.

"Come on, my beauty, we can do this," she urged Gypsy. "Only another few yards."

She reined Gypsy to a skidding stop alongside the cairn and reached for the marker planted in a hollow at head height, on top of the cairn. Shock tumbled through her as another hand clamped over it at the exact same second, their fingers tangling. "It's mine," she insisted, trying to wrest it from him.

She might as well have tried to wrestle a bear. He didn't release the marker but he did lift it clear of the hollow with her fingers still curled around it. "Looks like a draw to me."

Her breathing came in heaving gasps as she struggled to force words out. "Then the winner will be the first one back to the foot of the mountain."

He relinquished the marker. The sudden loss of contact with him was oddly disquieting, as if she'd lost something much more precious. She held the marker against her chest, fancying that it still held some of the warmth of his fingers.

Her breathing was unsteady but not only from the ride. "A draw, then."

He nodded. "For now."

There would be a lot of "for now" with this man, she sensed. While she was bound to a thousand years of tradition, he had only himself and the moment. What would it be like? Would it be exciting, a chance to reinvent yourself on a daily basis? Or would it be a solitary path, lacking foundations to build a future on?

The challenge was as close as she was likely to come to finding out. Up here she wasn't Princess Adrienne de Marigny, daughter of the ruling house of Carramer, but simply Dee, stretching herself to the limit in a test devised by the devil himself.

"Who thought up this ride, anyway?" Hugh asked, echoing her thoughts.

Tucking the marker into her boot top, she crossed her hands over the pommel and stared at the horizon. Gypsy dropped her head and began to crop grass. "For hundreds of years it was a coming-of-age ritual for Carramer boys. To prove they were men, they had to catch a wild horse, tame it and ride to the summit to collect a marker much like this. They were copied from an original dug up here. You can see it in the Nuee Museum."

"I can see why your menfolk didn't want women tackling this ride," he commented.

Her temper flared. She might have known he would remember her telling him that detail. "It was pure superstition, related to the gods the Mayat believed in. Do I need to remind you who reached the summit first?"

"I didn't say you aren't up to it," he said mildly. "Personally I think anyone who rides up here alone is bordering on crazy."

"You would have done it," she said.

He pushed his hat back on his head. A line of grime marked where it had been, she noticed idly, at the same time asking herself when he had begun to make such an impact on her. "You would have, too, if you'd lived back then, princess."

She felt as if she'd been read like a book. "How did you guess?"

He grinned. "You're the type to push yourself even when you don't have to."

She nodded. "Sometimes half the fun is knowing I don't have to."

His eyes narrowed as he studied her. "I guessed as much."

Her eyes widened. "How?"

His expansive gesture took in the vista around them. "You're here, aren't you? You didn't have to make this ride."

"You didn't leave me much choice if that land is to end up in the right hands," she reminded him.

A frown creased his rugged features. "It's already *in* the right hands, lady."

No one had *ever* called her lady before. Never. The sound of it, so normal and everyday, sent a charge through her. The stress of the ride must have made him forget who she was momentarily, making him treat her as he would any other woman.

Did he kiss other women the way he kissed her today? The thought doused the fire leaping inside her, his word serving as a timely reminder. She wasn't special to him, either as a princess or as a woman. If anything, she was a hindrance to his plans.

"Why did you kiss me?" she asked, needing to know as much as she had ever needed anything in her life.

He looked surprised, as if the question had caught him off guard. "Do I need a reason?"

"Men usually do."

"Have you been kissed by so many men, then?"

She was tempted to say yes, and bring the same watchful look into his eyes that she could feel in her own. But it wasn't true. Her untutored response to his kiss would have given her away in any case. She settled for "A few."

"All rich and titled, I'll bet."

The resentment she heard in his voice rankled. "Are most of the women in your life country bred and fond of horses?"

He looked puzzled. "Most of them. Why?"

"The men in mine are rich and titled. So what? It has as much to do with opportunity as personal preference."

"I see."

He saw but he didn't like it. She could tell by the sudden tightening of the muscles around his eyes and jawline. She cursed herself for reminding him of their differences when he had begun to treat her as an equal. Then she made herself face facts. They *were* from different worlds. Pretending otherwise was a recipe for disaster.

"Time for a rest," she said, springing to the ground. It gave slightly beneath her, rather like the ground underneath her when Hugh touched her, she thought. The sooner she got herself back onto solid ground, the better.

"We'd better not stay up here too long." He gestured toward the storm clouds gathering ominously on the horizon. Already many of the surrounding peaks had disappeared from view.

She had noticed the weather changing but, between the ride and Hugh's kisses, had been too preoccupied to worry about it. She was shocked to see the storm closing in so fast. "We should get out of here before the rain hits."

"Too late," he said, holding his hand out palm upward to catch the first fat drops of rain falling.

As if on cue, the heavens opened, dumping so much water so quickly that she was soaked through within minutes. The trees edging the summit plain, dense though they were, offered little shelter from the downpour.

She could see Hugh picturing what the rain would do to the trail. "We can walk the horses for a few hundred meters but we can't walk the whole way back," he said in confirmation. "And if this keeps up, it will be too treacherous to ride."

She went quiet. "I should have thought of that when I checked the forecast before we set off."

He tilted her chin and met her eyes. Rain streamed down her face like tears. He brushed some of it aside, and she shivered as his fingers touched her cheek. "It was a mutual decision, princess. Nobody's fault. So let's skip the guilt trip and start thinking. Is there an easier way to get off this mountain?"

She chewed her lower lip, not liking what she was thinking. "I don't know."

She had been read like a street sign, she saw when he frowned. "Yes, you do. Somebody has to bring the marker back up here, and I'm sure it isn't a ranger with a daredevil streak."

"It isn't. There is an easier way."

A deafening crack of thunder had her cowering against him. She wasn't normally afraid of storms, but she reacted instinctively to the loudness of this one. Hugh's arms came around her. He was as wet as she was, but she took comfort in being held against his hard body.

More than comfort. Arousal, she recognized as the unmistakable signals tore through her. She couldn't be. She was soaked to the skin, the lightning making her as skittish as the horses huddling beside them under the trees, their backs to the storm. Furthermore, she was a princess, she continued to lecture herself. Princesses didn't get turned on by men like Hugh.

But something was definitely happening here.

"Well?" he prompted. "Don't keep me in suspense."

For a mad moment she thought he had shared her feelings, but his stillness was only because he waited to hear her suggestion. "The alternative route is down the other side of the mountain and along the coast road," she said in a low voice. "The less intrepid tourists use it to visit the summit. It's safer but a lot longer."

"How much longer?"

"We wouldn't make it down off the mountain before nightfall."

Hugh weighed their options. They couldn't stay on top of the mountain and risk suffering exposure. Though Adrienne was tough she wasn't invincible, any more than he was. Held against him, he could already feel her shivering, although she was trying to keep it from him.

Trying to return the way they'd come was suicide. The going had been rough enough in the dry. In this downpour, it would be deadly. They'd been in the saddle for six hours already. They were good for another six but that was about it.

"This back way of yours, how long?" he asked.

"Under these conditions, maybe ten hours."

"We'd need somewhere dry to spend the night."

"There's a survival hut about halfway down the mountain, on the far side," she told him reluctantly.

He guessed this was the reason she'd hesitated. "And you don't fancy spending a night alone in it with me?"

The trouble was she *did* fancy it , as he put it, altogether too much. In spite of her arguments to herself about how ill-matched they were, some part of her wanted this day to last forever.

"It's hardly...appropriate." She grimaced as she used Lorne's favorite word.

"Worried about your brothers?"

More worried about herself, if truth be told. She chewed her lower lip. "Being out here during daylight hours is hardly the same as being here all night."

"No, it isn't."

She saw him reach into his pack. "Calling the cavalry?"

It was said in jest but to her surprise, he nodded. "Something of the sort."

When he turned, he had a state-of-the-art cell phone in one hand.

"Will it work in the mountains?" she asked, not sure whether she felt relieved or disappointed to find they weren't as isolated as she'd thought.

"It should. The cloud cover may make a difference. The battery's low but there ought to be enough juice for one quick call." He held the phone out to her. "You don't have to spend an uncomfortable night out here. Call your staff and tell them to send a chopper for you. If they don't waste time, they can land on the plain below us before the weather closes in completely."

"What about the horses?"

"They'll be okay on the summit while I help you down to meet the chopper. After you take off, I'll climb back up and take both horses down the long way. I can ride Avatar and lead Gypsy. If tourists use the trail, it must be fairly well marked."

She nodded, her thoughts whirling. But she didn't take the phone.

"Is something wrong?"

"What about the challenge?"

He looked angry. Had he hoped she wouldn't think of it until she had left the mountain, and he claimed victory by default? He soon disabused her. "Damn the challenge. Right now I'm more worried about your reputation if you end up spending a night out here with me."

In the face of his concern she immediately regretted being so suspicious. A knot of heat formed inside her. He must care, if her reputation was so important to him. What else might he feel toward her?

Fool, she told herself. Take the phone. Call for help and get the blazes out of here before you say or do something really crazy, like, "We started this together. I intend to stay and finish it."

"Are you out of your royal mind?"

Probably, she thought. Whatever the explanation, she felt herself come alive again. She was under no illusion it would be easy. Not in any way. But thoughts of the discomfort ahead paled beside the prospect of spending a night alone with Hugh.

He gestured again with the phone. "Last chance to change your mind."

She thought again about her brothers. They would be angry enough when they heard about the ride. The storm around them now would hardly compare with Lorne's fury if she was out all night with Hugh. She'd hate it to affect his business dealings with the princes.

"You haven't said anything about how the challenge could affect your business with my brothers," she said.

"Why should it have any effect? I don't plan on losing."

"I meant on your relationship with Michel."

"I doubt he'll be thrilled, but since you came of your own free will, it shouldn't affect our business dealings one way or the other. In my experience, as long as two men respect each other, they can do business regardless of their feelings. So don't worry on my account. Think of your own reputation," Hugh urged.

She couldn't imagine Michel *not* respecting Hugh. "You're right," she said on a sighing breath and reached for the cell phone. As she took it from him, their fingers brushed, and she felt the now-familiar jolt of awareness arrow along her arm and bury itself somewhere around her heart. It made what she was about to do all the more fool-hardy, but somehow, more necessary.

She flipped the phone open and punched in the direct number that would connect her with Cindy Cook. Her assistant answered almost at once. "Cindy, it's me. I'll talk quickly because I don't know how long the battery of this phone will last. I just want you to know I'm perfectly fine and being looked after, so there's no need to worry about me. But I won't be back until sometime tomorrow." A pause. "No, I don't know exactly when."

Hugh's growl of objection clashed with the phone's low-battery signal. "Yes, reschedule my appointments. Tell them—" Her eyes met Hugh's over the top of the phone. His eyes burned and a muscle worked in his cheek. "—tell them something unexpected came up."

She gasped as he wrenched the instrument from her. "Tell them she'll be back by nightfall if you get a helicopter up here pronto," Hugh said, but found himself talking into a useless phone. He glared at Adrienne. "What in blazes do you think you're doing?"

She reverted to princess mode. "Kindly don't swear at me."

"That isn't swearing. *This* is swearing." He let loose with a string of words she hadn't even known were in the dictionary. Come to think of it, they probably weren't.

She let the air sizzle for a few minutes. "Finished?"

"Princess, I haven't even started."

He rammed the now-dead phone into a pocket and pulled her against him, his mouth descending on hers with unerring accuracy. She got the sense that it was either kiss her or kill her as the fiery pressure of his lips urged hers apart, allowing him to plunder the moist cavern of her mouth.

As his tongue tangled with hers, she grew lightheaded but felt her pulses leap. He had intended to show her how dangerously she was living, but instead she felt more alive than ever before. The rain could pour forever if it meant she could hang on to the exquisite sensations coiling through her at his touch.

He was angry. She felt that, too, radiating from his body to hers as if they were linked by a high-energy beam. That his anger was on her account, because she wouldn't let him protect her, filled her with elation.

Kissing wasn't supposed to be amusing, she knew. But what he made her feel was so wonderful and unstoppable, that she began to shake with suppressed laughter.

He lifted his head and glared down at her. "You think this is funny, princess?"

From somewhere, she recalled that the worst thing a woman could do was belittle a man's prowess at seduction. She hadn't meant to. In Hugh's case, it would have been a miscarriage of justice, because he kissed the way she had always dreamed of being kissed. No doubt he made love just as skillfully.

She hastily reined in her runaway imagination. "I wasn't laughing at you, or your technique."

His eyes narrowed. "You don't know the first thing about my technique. In fact, I'll bet you don't know about any man's...technique." He stretched the word out, loading it with unmistakable innuendo. "Am I right?"

Now she was the one to feel slighted. "If you're asking have I ever been with a man..."

His hands tightened on her shoulders. "Have you?"

"Of course not."

He gave her a slight shake, although he looked as if he'd like to do a lot more. "You say it as if it's perfectly normal, when you're probably the first twenty-three-year-old virgin I've ever met."

The contrast in their experience emphasized the gulf between them. "As a princess, I have to consider my reputation."

"Exactly my point," he said on a note of exasperation. "You can't be such an innocent as not to know that spending a night alone in the forest with man is playing with fire?"

Her urge to laugh vanished as she faced a simple, unavoidable fact. "I trust you, Hugh. With my life."

"It may come to that." He released her and began to pace in a small circle beneath the dripping trees. "I can't believe that winning this contest is more important to you than anything else, including your reputation."

How could one man be so blind? Of course she wanted to win, but a sense of responsibility had also been drummed into her from childhood. How could she live with herself if she abandoned him on the mountain in dangerous weather and something happened to him? That her reasons might be far more personal, she didn't want to consider, at least not now.

"This has nothing to do with the contest," she said flatly, hurt that he obviously thought it did.

His skeptical look raked her. "Yeah, right. Next thing you'll be telling me you're spending a night on a rain-soaked mountain with me from choice."

It *was* her choice, but nothing she could say would make him believe that winning the contest wasn't the reason. "You're right," she said heavily, putting all her hurt feelings into words, only not the ones she really wanted to say. "I'm staying because I want that land so badly I'll do anything to get it. I want to keep Carazzan and I want you gone from my country and my life. There, are you satisfied?"

"Only a twenty-three-year-old virgin as beautiful and desirable as you could ask a man that and not already know the answer." Considering she had just told him what he expected to hear, he seemed more angry than pleased, she thought. What did he want from her?

He took her arm and she jumped. He gave her a scathing look. "Relax, I may not be royal, but I know how to behave like a gentleman. After tonight your reputation may be in shreds, but it won't be on my account. I just hope the prize turns out to be worth it and you know what you're doing."

That made two of them, she thought as she followed him.

Chapter Seven

The heavy rain had made the clay surface slick as ice, and it was a challenge to make any progress at all on the so-called easier route down the far side of the mountain. Two steps forward and one step back was the best they could do.

Adrienne tried to be glad they were going downhill, but the slippery track made it even more daunting. The sense of disapproval she felt pouring from Hugh didn't help. He thought she had insisted on staying because she wanted to win the contest. She couldn't tell him the real reason, knowing he wouldn't thank her for sacrificing herself on his account.

It didn't feel like a sacrifice, it felt right, she thought, with no clear idea why. If she had any sense, she would be in a helicopter by now, on her way back to her safe, warm country house, instead of slogging through mud alongside a man who didn't want her with him in the first place. Perversely she knew she wouldn't trade her present situation for all the luxury in the world.

She began to envy the horses the extra traction their four legs provided. Riding was out of the question, and her legs ached before they'd covered even a mile toward the survival hut marked on the map. If this was the easy route, she was glad they hadn't tried to go back the way they'd come.

Hugh helped her across yet another fallen log blocking the trail. "You say tourists come up this way? They must be crazy."

She gave him a smile she knew was wan at best, determined not to let him see how tired she was. He would only say, I told you so. "Where's your sense of adventure?"

He frowned. "Probably left at the same place you left yours."

She lifted her chin. "I'm not ready to admit defeat yet."

"Somehow I didn't think you would be."

Hugh was furious with her, but he had to admire her courage. Mud spattered, soaked and obviously exhausted, she still gave as good as she got. He tried to imagine Jemima slogging through ankle-deep mud with her sense of humor intact. He failed.

The princess had good reason to persevere, he reminded himself. She had as much at stake as he did, more if you counted the flak she'd get from her brothers if they heard about this adventure.

Why hadn't she left when he gave her the chance? Give his ex-wife a cell phone and she'd have been out of here before the echo died. Yet the princess, with the best excuse in the world, had chosen to stay. It couldn't be for his sake, so that left the land, and Carazzan.

He hadn't thought much about the prize horse for hours, he realized in some astonishment. Ever since Jemima's stunt stopped him from buying Carazzan, the need to track the horse down and try to set things right had occupied some part of his thoughts for months.

Now Adrienne was the one keeping his mind busy. He had to make a conscious effort to focus on negotiating the trail safely. The rain had eased off, but it had made the going slow and dangerous. One slip and someone, human or animal, could end up hundreds of feet down a ravine.

A chill fluttered along his spine as he imagined Adrienne slipping over the edge. He wasn't aware that his hold on her arm tightened until she let out a soft cry. "You're hurting me, Hugh."

He eased off but he didn't let go. "They're going to find out, you know."

She gave him a confused look. The mud on her face made her look impossibly young and innocent. From somewhere he dredged up a memory of one of his earlier foster mothers dabbing water onto the corner of a handkerchief and cleaning the grime from his face with it. For the first time, he understood the instinct.

"Who'll find out what?"

"Your brothers are bound to find out about this."

"Because you intend to tell them?"

The hurt in her eyes and voice cut him to his core. "Good grief, no. What would I have to gain?"

"You tell me."

It wouldn't get him Carazzan, if that was what she thought he meant. It was far more likely to get him thrown out of the country on his ear. "I have nothing to gain from betraying you," he said carefully, finding he wanted to shake her to make her understand. His hands bunched into fists at his sides with the strain of keeping them to himself. "But your absence is bound to cause talk, and gossip travels a lot faster than we're doing right now."

"My staff are completely trustworthy," she said grimly.

"I thought mine were, too, until one of my most trusted people helped cover up the fact that my ex-wife was holed up in Paris with another man."

He thought of all the phone calls home while he was traveling around the South Pacific. At the time it didn't strike him as odd that the only times he connected with Jemima directly were when she called him. The rest of the time he was told she was out shopping, in the shower, sleeping, anything but the truth. He hoped his trust in Adrienne wasn't equally misplaced.

"Did you love her very much?"

Her obvious concern made him uncomfortable for some reason. "I thought I did, but this isn't the Carramer equivalent of the Foreign Legion so there's no need to look so tragic."

"The end of love is always tragic."

"You'd know, of course."

He'd hurt her, he saw from the shadows that immediately darkened her beautiful eyes. He hadn't meant to, but he didn't want her to care about him. It wasn't part of their deal, and it reminded him uncomfortably of how much he could care for her if things had been different.

She brushed rain from her face, the droplets looking like tears. But there was fire in her voice as she said, "I may be inexperienced, but that doesn't mean I don't know what love is."

A pang shot through him, catching him off guard. He found he didn't like thinking of her in the arms of any other man, even though his arms were off-limits. He felt a driving need to change the subject. "We may have to spend the night out here, but isn't it a cliché to start exchanging life stories?"

"What would you rather talk about? Horse breeding? Bloodlines?"

"Hell, no." He hadn't meant to snap, but discussing reproduction of any kind with her seemed reckless when they had the whole night to get through.

She misunderstood his reaction. "Because it would remind you of Carazzan? I'd forgotten how much you want that horse."

The odd thing was, so had he. Once, he would have said Carazzan was the most important thing in the world to him. Now he wasn't so sure. When did his single-minded pursuit of the dream to produce the world's greatest riding horse start to seem insufficient? He was afraid the answer was no more than an arm's length away.

He drove the thought off. "Do we have to talk at all? Saving our energy for the trail makes more sense."

She spun around to face him, sprays of mud flying from her boots. "Is it all women, or just me?"

It was his turn to look confused. "Excuse me?"

"I'm sorry your ex-wife had an affair and that you were evidently hurt by it. But hating all women isn't going to change anything."

"What makes you think I hate all women?"

"Don't you?"

She tempted him to prove her wrong in the most physical way. Mud splattered, half dropping with tiredness, her gorgeous hair tugging free of its fetters to cling around her face in damp curls, she still looked magnificent.

Kissing her to show how wrong she was seemed far too enticing a prospect. He made himself turn away and focus on the mist-shrouded view.

She took his silence for an answer. "Then it must be me you dislike. Is it because of my position?"

He didn't turn around, afraid that if he did, nothing would stop him from taking her in his arms. "It doesn't exactly help."

"You mean if I was an ordinary woman, you would find me attractive?"

"I find you attractive now." If she only knew how much. This time he did turn around. "But you're not an ordinary woman, and no matter how much we pretend, that isn't going to change."

Her head came up, and defiance shone in her eyes. "I don't want it to change."

Not even for him. He heard the part she didn't say. He was right, she was Jemima all over again, happy to play at being ordinary. And like her, when it came to the crunch, the princess wouldn't willingly give up any of the trappings of her station. He had known it since their first meeting, but it still hurt to have the truth thrown in his face. "So why all the business of pretending to be Dee?"

"You really don't understand, do you? It's a holiday, a chance to see my world through different eyes."

"And so is this." His gesture took in the dripping forest around them and the ice-slick clay of the trail under their feet. "It isn't reality and it never can be. I can't change who I am and you've just said you don't want to."

"So it comes back to being my fault."

He took her by the shoulders. "It's nobody's fault, damn it, it just is."

For a moment frozen in time he stared into her eyes, drowning in them. His gaze went to her full lips. Her tongue darted out to lick them as if they felt dry suddenly, and it was almost his undoing. He wanted to kiss her so badly he ached inside.

Since he had just explained why it was impossible, he wouldn't let himself give in to the urge. Less than gently he spun her around and started her down the slope again. She steadied herself by gripping a handful of Gypsy's mane. Hugh felt like a brute.

Couldn't she see that this was going to be much harder on her than on him? In spite of her confidence in her staff, he wasn't sure they could hush this up, although he hoped so for her sake. If it came to the crunch, he could deal with anything the media could throw at him. They'd had a field day with him after Jemima had called one of her pet columnists and unleashed the story of his supposed insolvency. He hadn't enjoyed it, but he knew he could handle it.

Royalty was used to being in the spotlight, but even so, he doubted if Adrienne was prepared for the kind of feeding frenzy that would occur if word got out of how she'd spent this night. He suspected that her brothers' wrath would be mild by comparison.

Adrienne faltered and would have slipped if he hadn't caught her by one arm and hauled her back upright, then rescued Gypsy's reins when they slid from her grasp. He handed them back to her. "Would you like to stop and rest?"

She shivered, but whether with exposure or something more personal, he couldn't tell. "Thank you, but I'm fine. It's not much farther to the hut."

He had wanted coolness between them, so he could hardly complain when he got it. "If these maps you supplied are accurate, it's only another half mile. Think you'll make it?"

"I'll make it."

She didn't add *if it killed her* because she didn't want to provoke any more outbursts of concern from him. She was close to exhausted, and tears welled very near the surface. It wouldn't take much for her to break down in front of him, and she was damned if she'd give him the satisfaction.

His claim that they could never mean anything to each other because of who and what they were was probably accurate. She still doubted if it was the whole story. His ex-wife had hurt him badly, she had seen in the way he talked about it. He might have dismissed it as over and done with, but he wasn't fooling her.

Hugh was keeping something back, she knew. Maybe tonight when they were alone in the survival hut, he might open up a little more, but she doubted it. For some reason he wanted to keep an emotional wall between them. For all she knew, it was a good thing. So why didn't it feel like one?

She hated to think Carazzan was the reason. They had started out as rivals over the horse, but she had begun to think they could be friends when this was over. Maybe even the partners he had proposed at the start. If she hadn't been so stubborn, wanting it all, they wouldn't be in this fix now.

She had put on a good face for Hugh, but she was troubled by the thought of her brothers' reaction. In theory she was of age and could do as she pleased; in fact, as a princess, she was bound by her allegiance to Lorne as ruler of Carramer to follow his wishes. She was sure they wouldn't include spending a night alone in the forest with a guest of the royal family.

There was nothing to be done about it now so she forced herself to focus on putting one foot in front of the other, aware of Hugh moving quietly back to her side, his hair-trigger reflexes set to catch her if she looked in danger of slipping again. It was a pity his safety net didn't extend to her emotions, as well.

When the trail gave way to a clearing, she wanted to weep with relief. By the failing light they found their way to the small hut at its center. Adrienne was grateful for the dim light, thinking that in full daylight she would shudder at the thought of spending a night in such a place. In this light it looked cozy and inviting.

Since most of the visitors using the trail traveled by

horseback, the hut's provisions included feed for Gypsy and Avatar. A three-sided structure made an adequate stable for the night. The horses seemed glad to be out of the cold.

Adrienne shared the feeling. She had volunteered to see to the horses while Hugh got a fire going in the hut. When she came in, he was crouched at it, feeding kindling to the flames. There wasn't much warmth yet but the sight of the flames lifted her spirits. Or was it the sight of him, primitive man bringing fire to his woman, that fired her with inexplicable pleasure?

She forced the feeling away. "Is there any light?"

"Only a spirit lamp, but there's plenty of spare fuel."

She found it and stared at it until he came and took the lamp from her hands. "You've never camped out before, have you?"

"Yes, I have."

"Where and when?"

"On Isle des Anges as a child. We spent a week under canvas at the beach. That was camping."

"No servants?"

She flinched from the censure in his voice. "Only a couple. Someone had to make the beds up and cook the food."

He gave a long-suffering sigh. "It seems we have very different ideas of what constitutes camping. You remind me of a friend back home who says his wife's idea of roughing it is to turn off her side of the electric blanket."

"Very funny." He was determined to see her as spoiled and useless. Well then, she would be spoiled and useless. What was the point of trying to show him she was different?

She kept her back straight as she went to the wide bed made up on a shelf against one wall. When she sat down on it, the unyielding surface promised an uncomfortable night. There was only the one bed and that promised even greater discomfort since they plainly couldn't share it.

"What are we eating?" she asked in her most imperious tone.

He gave her a scathing look. "Whatever you're cooking."

She tossed her head, her hair flying around her face. "I'm the useless one, remember? I don't cook, either."

"Then we don't eat, either."

"Don't tell me you're one of those male chauvinists who think cooking is a job for women only?"

"I won't tell you, because I don't believe it. But this is a survival hut, not the Ritz, and there's no room service. I'll be busy rounding up enough wood to keep the fire going through the night so we don't freeze to death. That leaves you to do the cooking."

Normally she would have accepted it as a reasonable division of labor, but his attitude made her so furious that she was damned if she'd touch the heavy cast iron implements that passed for cooking tools. A supply of canned goods came with the hut, and they would leave a donation with the ranger to replenish what they used, so they needn't go hungry, but that didn't solve the question of who was to prepare the meal.

Hugh seemed to be in no doubt. He picked up an ax from a corner. "You should have a meal ready by the time I'm back with some wood."

Who did he think she was, Annie Oakley? she asked herself, dredging up the only woman's name associated with the American frontier she could remember. Annie Oakley had been handy with a gun, she also recalled. Adrienne smiled as she imagined any man forcing Oakley to cook. She'd probably have shot his—

She jumped as Hugh's face appeared at the door again.

"Time's wasting," he said with infuriating good humor. Most men would have quailed in the face of the royal glare of displeasure she aimed at him. He didn't seem to notice it.

As the minutes ticked by, she listened for the sound of the ax falling but could hear nothing over the howl of the wind through the trees. Suddenly her behavior seemed pointless. Acting like a spoiled child would only confirm Hugh's beliefs about her, not change them, she thought.

With a sigh she got up and reached for the heavy frying pan. Hugh had taken it for granted that she knew what to do with it. She did, but like her understanding of sex, it was all theory. She had never actually cooked a meal in her life.

She scanned the shelf of canned foods, choosing one with a ring-pull opener because she wasn't sure how she'd cope with a can opener that didn't work on electricity. As she levered the lid off, a fingernail cracked. She regarded the broken nail in dismay. Coming on top of everything else, it was almost the last straw. She wanted nothing more than to sit down and cry.

But that would only prove to Hugh that she was as useless as he suspected, so she took a steadying breath and studied the contents of the can. Tomatoes flavored with herbs. Dumping them into the pan, she pulled down another can, finding some kind of meat this time. It landed in a lump in the middle of the tomatoes, splattering juice. It was hardly *haute cuisine*, but the combination looked vaguely edible. She carried the pan to the fire and set it on the flames.

Then she turned to her pack, rummaging through it for a nail file. Worrying about a fingernail seemed foolish, given the state of the rest of her, but since it was the only thing she could repair right now, she felt driven to try.

"What the devil?"

Hugh shot past her and yanked the pan off the flames, yelping as the cast iron handle seared his palm. The meat had caught fire, she saw, before he clamped a lid over the pan to douse the leaping flames. "Are you trying to burn the place down?"

She drew herself up regally, not letting him see how close the tears of exhaustion and frustration were. "I was doing the best I could."

Putting the pan down on the table beside the nail file she'd just unpacked, he eyed it in disgust. "The best for yourself, obviously."

His judgmental attitude was the last straw. "How was I to know the food would catch fire so quickly?"

"By watching it instead of worrying about your looks. This isn't called a survival hut for nothing."

"We're not really in danger."

"We could be if you burn the hut down and leave us without shelter for the night."

"My fault again," she snapped. "It seems where you're concerned I can do nothing right, so I might as well stop trying."

She spun away but he was faster, his hand closing around her wrist with lightning speed. She snapped back as if on a leash. "Not so fast. I didn't figure you for a woman who gives up easily."

She glared at the strong fingers coiled around her wrist. It should have been a signal to release her, but it had absolutely no effect on him. "I haven't given up. I still intend to win this contest."

"Who's talking about the contest?"

"We have nothing else to talk about, as you've proven time and time again."

He shook his head in silent negation. "Nothing but this."

In the dancing flames his face was all hard planes and angles, his eyes black pools in their deep sockets. As he drew her against him, she shivered but not with fear. Not even her inexperience could mistake the need leaping through her for anything else. Or blind her to the desire she saw in his gaze.

At some level she had known it would come to this as soon as he suggested taking the long way back. He must have known it, too. Perhaps his eagerness to airlift her off the mountain had been an attempt to stop it from happening.

It wouldn't have made any difference, she thought. What was between them could only be delayed, not stopped. If she had left, he would have come after her. Sooner or later she would have ended up right where she was, in his strong embrace, every sense she possessed singing a siren song of need.

Fight it, push him away, retreat behind your wall of royal reserve, she told herself. Just because it felt good didn't make it right. He disliked everything she was, everything she stood for. If all they shared was passion, how could it ever be enough?

Images of her brothers and their families flashed through her mind. She wanted love on the same terms, as a package with babies and a future, everything Hugh didn't seem to want. His own history as an unwanted child made him wary of commitment, she sensed. He blamed it on choosing the wrong wife, but had he chosen her precisely because the relationship was unlikely to last?

If it were true, Adrienne was a fool to think things would be any different with her.

But when he covered her mouth in a long, soul-searing kiss, she couldn't help herself. She responded out of primal need, kissing him back until she felt drained of emotion and hungry for replenishment. She let her fingers tangle in his hair, pulling his head down to deepen the kiss. Still it wasn't enough.

It felt better when he freed her shirt and eased his hands under it. She knew a moment of anxiety when he unhooked her bra a little too expertly, but when he slid his hands under the creamy fullness of her breasts, his touch banished all reason.

A low moan was ripped from her as he left her mouth and skimmed the side of her neck and along the line of her shoulder. Another moan as he found a hollow at the side of her throat and kissed there, too. She felt the pulse point erupt into frantic beating at the searing touch.

She let her head drop back, needing air. "Why are you doing this?"

"It's a gift for us both. A reward for what we went through to get this far."

"You got us here safely. I only tried to set fire to us."

Under her shirt his fingers closed around her nipples, and heat poured through her. "News for you, princess. You succeeded."

Her breathing felt unsteady. Her legs weren't far behind, she thought, clasping both arms around him to try to ground herself. Dangerous move, she discovered as she was pressed hard against him.

She should have expected it, but the extent of his arousal sent shock waves through her. He sensed the change immediately, and his questing mouth slowed although he kept up the gentle, irresistible kneading of her breasts until she could hardly breathe. "You had to know what you're doing to me," he rasped.

It couldn't begin to compare with what he was doing to her, she thought in a daze of sensations she feared as much as she craved them. She put her hands to his shoulders, but it was like trying to move Mount Mayat. "I wasn't...I didn't—"

"You don't want this?" He bent his head and took one breast into his mouth, the sensation so exquisite that she almost fainted. "Or this?" He flicked his tongue over the nipple in lightning-quick, teasing strokes.

"Yes...no." How could she think straight when he kept doing that?

He heard the confusion in her voice and straightened, his chest rising and falling in time with his labored breathing as he said, "It can't be both, princess. You have to tell me what you want."

She wasn't the only one fighting for breath, she noticed, knowing it had nothing to do with the altitude. She wanted him with every fiber of her being, craved his touch more than she had ever wanted anything. Nothing that felt so right could possibly be wrong, she told herself, reaching a decision. She lifted her face to him. "I want you to kiss me again, Hugh."

His gaze lingered on her mouth for the longest time, as if he was sorely tempted to comply. Then he turned away and placed both palms flat against the rough-hewn table. His shoulders were rigid with tension.

She swallowed bitter disappointment. "What is it?"

He didn't turn around. "You want me to kiss you again, but I don't think you understand where it has to end if I do."

"Of course I understand," she snapped. "I'm not such an innocent as all that."

When he turned, he was back in control—barely, she saw. She felt the strongest urge to throw herself into his arms and snap his control as he had shattered hers. Then reject him as he seemed determined to do to her.

"Knowing and doing are hardly the same thing," he said as if in confirmation.

It was exactly why she had wanted him to make love to her, because she would finally *know*. Some part of her already did know, she recognized, some genetic inheritance that went all the way back to Eve. But that part hadn't conceived of *Hugh*, the man she—good grief, she had almost added to herself *the man she loved*.

It couldn't be true, could it? She wanted Hugh to make love to her to satisfy the yearnings he had aroused in her, not because she was in love with him. Too much stood between them for any such thing to make sense.

As if she wasn't already aware of it, he said, "You'll have enough explaining to do when we get back as it is, without adding more complications."

So he thought of making love to her as a complication. She shouldn't be surprised to hear him put it into words, but it still hurt more than she would have dreamed possible. This time it was easy to withdraw behind her wall of royal reserve, because it was the only defense she had left.

"I'm sorry you see me as a *complication*." She spat the word out.

"That isn't what I meant and you know it."

All she knew was the pain of offering herself to him and being rejected. For someone used to having the red carpet rolled out wherever she went, it was hard to take, she accepted with scrupulous honesty. Was that what was bothering her?

No, she was bothered because she had never offered herself to any man before. Had never wanted to before. To have her gift thrown back at her hurt worse than anything she had ever experienced.

"Kindly leave me alone," she said, managing to summon a tone of royal command.

Anger flared in his expression. "In case you haven't noticed, princess, this cabin doesn't have any spare rooms I can retreat to."

"Please," she tried again on a note barely above a whisper.

Something in her face must have told him how much she needed time alone. He relented. "I'll bring in the rest of the firewood."

As soon as the door closed behind him, she crumpled onto the bed and rested her head in her hands. What a fool she was, thinking there could be anything but rivalry between them. She already knew he had no time for her. She was too new to lovemaking to satisfy him. She was also cast in the same mold as his ex-wife. At some level he could be seeking revenge for his failed marriage without realizing it, and Adrienne had unwittingly provided the means. It didn't stop her from aching with unfulfilled desire.

Telling herself that there was no future in it didn't help. She remembered the public displeasure that had greeted Lorne's decision to marry an Australian. It had ended in tragedy when she died in a car accident. Then he had fallen in love with Allie, another Australian, but as different from his first wife as…as Adrienne and Hugh, she thought.

There any similarity ended, Adrienne thought bitterly. Allie and Lorne's love was so vibrant that Carramer had taken her into its collective heart right away. She had paved the way for the people's acceptance of an American as Michel's bride, both women fitting easily into their roles as royal consorts.

Adrienne couldn't imagine Hugh doing any such thing. He was already wedded to his ranching life and his dream of breeding the perfect horse. She couldn't conceive of him fulfilling royal duties at her side. And she couldn't change

who she was any more than she could change the weather
on Mount Mayat.

The only alternative would be to let him take the lead,
but her plans didn't include being ruled by any man. She'd
had enough of that with two brothers who thought they
knew what was best for her.

Slowly she lifted her head, summoning a reserve of defiance from deep within. She had had plenty of practice at
hiding her feelings in public. She could hide them from
Hugh now and at least walk away from this with her self-
respect intact.

Before he could hurt her, she had to care what he
thought, she reminded herself. And she didn't. She definitely didn't love him. By the time he returned with his
arms full of firewood, she had almost made herself believe
it.

Chapter Eight

In the clearing outside the hut, Hugh attacked the logs with the fervor of a man possessed. In the dim light he could barely see to aim the ax, but he had to burn away his frustration before he went back inside and did something they'd both regret.

Again and again the blade whistled down until his muscles screamed in protest. Good. It would stop his thoughts straying back to Adrienne. The tactic worked for all of ten seconds at a time before she was back in his mind. Tonight she didn't look like a princess. She looked as messy as a woman who'd woken up in the morning after a sensational night of lovemaking. She looked gorgeous.

But she *was* a princess and innocent, as well. The thought of being her first lover took his breath away as he imagined how special and memorable he would like to make it for her. Her response to his kisses suggested she was a fast learner. It wouldn't be long before they reached out and touched the stars together.

He wasn't usually poetic, and it was misplaced this time,

he thought, aiming another savage blow at the log. The ax caught and he wrenched it free, welcoming the struggle as a way to divert his runaway thoughts, but they turned back to her as soon as he swung the blade high again. In the first place, she was out of his class. One such ill-fated union should be enough to last him a lifetime.

In the second place, she'd had her future mapped out for her from the day she was born. It didn't include marriage to a foreign rancher with no pedigree he could trace. With grim humor he pictured a church with generations of family crowding the bride's side and empty pews on the groom's. That was reality.

All the same he couldn't help remembering the hurt clouding her eyes when he pushed her away. Dammit, why couldn't she understand why he couldn't take from her what she had been more than willing to give? There was no point in Hugh trying to explain it to her. After years of having decisions made for her by her brothers, she wouldn't thank Hugh for making this one on her behalf, even though it was for her own good.

Slam. The blade hit a knot in the wood, the shock jarring all the way to his shoulder. Knowing when he was beaten, he tossed the ax aside and began to gather the wood he'd already split. He'd found the uncut logs in a lean-to shelter beside the hut, so they were reasonably dry. Otherwise, it would have been a long, cold night.

Fire or no fire, he was in for a cold night, he reflected. Only knowing he was doing the right thing made it possible to go inside and act as if nothing was wrong.

His resolve wavered when he found her leaning over the table, her jodhpurs stretched taut, outlining her delectable shape. Traces of her perfume mingled with the smell of cooking, making him nostalgic for a homecoming he'd never really known except in imagination. His arms throbbed with the need to hold her. Resolutely he crossed them over his chest.

It was just as well. While he was chopping firewood, she'd turned back into a princess again. He saw this from the haughty angle of her head and the oh-so-cool look she bestowed on him when she turned with the frying pan in her hands. He tried to tell himself it was for the best.

"I rescued dinner. It wasn't too badly burned," she said, avoiding his eyes. "Once I scraped off the black bits, the rest looked all right."

Say something , anything, he commanded himself, aware that what he wanted to say had no place between them. Words like *I love you*. He silenced them by force of will. Wanting her wasn't the same as loving her, he told himself.

He had given his trust too often in his life and knew where it got him. Foster parents and foster siblings, Big Dan Jordan, Jemima. Of them all, only Big Dan had delivered on his promises, but he'd hurt Hugh in the end, too. It wasn't his foster father's fault that he'd had a bad heart, but, however irrational, Hugh's grief and sense of abandonment still ran deep.

He settled for saying, "This should last us through the night," as he dumped the split logs into a bin beside the fireplace.

She barely glanced at the logs. "Good."

She put a plate of food on the table near him, then sat down as far away from him as possible. He reached for the plate and a spoon. He should welcome the distance between them and admire her strength of character for providing it. Instead he felt empty and alone.

You can't have it both ways, pal, he thought as he ate, more hungry than he had realized. She's not for you, so be glad she's making it easy for you to stay away. Somehow the argument wasn't as persuasive as it should have been.

"I must be hungry because this stuff isn't bad," he commented, mopping up the last of the tomato juice with half a sandwich left over from their lunch. He set the plate aside. "I must remember to 'flame' grill all my meals in future."

Still hurting from his rejection, she had trouble seeing the funny side. "I'm glad you put out the fire in time." He had certainly done it in her.

"Only the top was singed," he confirmed, seemingly unaware of her inner turmoil. "The rest tasted fine."

The meal was appalling and he probably knew it, but this was no time to be choosy. Was that how he saw her? Adrienne hated to think so but it seemed possible. If they hadn't been alone in the wilderness, would desire have flamed so incandescently between them so quickly? She would never know.

Hiding her distress behind a pose of royal dignity, she picked up the plates and carried them to a tiny stainless steel sink in one corner. At least she knew what washing-up implements were for. Hugh watched but made no move to help. She was glad. It was easier to maintain an aloof air when he wasn't near her.

When she turned on the tap, the water ran rust-red. "Let it run for a few seconds to clear the pipes," Hugh suggested. "With all this rain we don't have to worry about draining the rainwater tank."

She threw a dish towel at him. "You could make yourself useful instead of giving me orders."

He snatched the cloth out of the air. "You're ready enough to give me orders, princess."

"Don't call me that. The correct form of address is 'Your Highness' at first meeting and 'ma'am' thereafter."

Anger had prompted her to put him in his place, but she regretted it as soon as she saw his face. It was as blank as a stone wall, but behind it she sensed his simmering fury.

When had she come to read him so well? They'd known each other for all of a week, but his mask of indifference didn't fool her. Well, turnabout was fair play, she thought. He was the one who had rejected her for being who and what she was. He could hardly blame her for living up to his expectations.

Without a word he stalked to the sink and began to dry the plates as she handed them to him. He dried them as if he would prefer to break something instead.

Carried out in silence, cleaning up took almost no time, and she looked around for something else to do, anything to take her mind off their situation. He misread her glance. "It's all right, you can take the bed. I'll sleep on the floor tonight."

She hadn't given a thought to the sleeping arrangements, although she should have, given the way his kisses had driven her thinking. She had been too busy nursing her wounded feelings. Now she looked around the cabin, really seeing its limitations for the first time.

About twelve feet by nine, it had one window and a bare wooden floor. A wide shelf across one end accommodated a mattress heaped with army blankets and a pile of pillows. At the other end was the fireplace, and in between were two straight-backed wooden chairs and the rough-hewn table. The supplies were on a shelf above it. There wasn't even a couch he could sleep on.

With the coming of night, the storm had gathered strength again, and she could hear raindrops spattering against the window. The wind whistled through a crack under the door. Sharing the bed was the only thing that made sense. Knowing he didn't want to make love to her should simplify everything. Yet her relief was mingled with disappointment.

Why didn't she let him sleep on the floor and be done

with it? If he spent an uncomfortable night, she would have an advantage on the final leg of the challenge tomorrow. Her innate sense of fair play won. Angry as she was with him, she couldn't let him risk pneumonia. "We'll share the bed. It's plenty big enough."

His hard gaze swept from the bed back to her. "There's no need to go overboard with the noblesse oblige, ma'am."

His emphatic use of the title grated, although he was following her instructions. "This has nothing to do with nobility, I'm being practical. You won't be in any shape to finish the ride if you come down with something."

"All the same, I'll take the floor."

Was she such a disappointment that he couldn't bear sharing a bed with her for one night, even platonically? She resolved to show him it worked both ways. She would share the bed with him if it killed her. But she couldn't help wondering if she needed to prove something to him or to herself.

She spread her hands wide. "Oh, well, if you're afraid you can't control yourself…"

She let the challenge hang in the air, savoring the change she saw in his face. He looked angry and disbelieving by turns. "You really do believe in playing with fire, don't you, Your Highness?"

"According to you, it won't *be* playing with fire. You've made it clear that you don't find me attractive, so there's no harm in sharing the sleeping platform is there?"

The slow, assessing look he gave her stirred her senses. "What makes you think I don't find you attractive?"

Just not attractive enough, she thought, still finding it hard to be grateful for his restraint. Harder still to accept that what he made her feel was so one-sided. "You have a strange way of showing it."

"If I followed my instincts, I wouldn't have to show you.

Nor would we need to discuss who gets the bed, because we'd both be in it right now.'' He gestured toward the leaping flames. ''And keeping warm would be the least of our problems.''

Heat clawed through her, more from the picture his words painted in her mind than from the open fire. She struggled to subdue the emotions threatening her self-control. She was a princess, for pity's sake, schooled from childhood to appear unruffled no matter what. Except that no part of her training had anticipated Hugh.

She went to the hearth and fussed with the fire, more to give herself time to regain control than because she knew what she was doing. When Hugh took the poker from her hands and their fingers touched, she jumped.

''You're going the right way to put it out altogether,'' he informed her.

If only her emotions could be extinguished so easily. She took refuge in annoyance. ''You have no right to tell me what I can and can't do.''

He curled her fingers around the poker again and stepped back. ''Fine. We'll do it your way. Wreck the fire if you want to, but don't expect me to build it up again if you wake up freezing during the night.''

His male chauvinism triggered unwelcome memories of her brothers, and she shot him a disdainful look. ''You think I don't know how to make a fire?''

''I don't think, I know. You're wielding that poker like a dueling sword.''

''Maybe I've had more practice with a sword than a poker.'' As it happened, it was true. Fencing had been one of the skills her tutors considered a princess should master.

''Now, that I'd like to see,'' Hugh murmured, his gaze softening. ''The warrior princess wielding her sword.''

''You sound as if you don't believe me,'' she said haughtily, as much because she suspected that he wasn't making fun of her as because she feared he was. He was her rival, she reminded herself urgently. She wanted to dislike him, but when these fragments of closeness bloomed between them, it became harder and harder. She found herself remembering the feel of his strong hands and the promise she had tasted when he kissed her.

A promise he didn't intend to keep, she told herself, fighting the knot of frustrated need that clenched inside.

He inclined his head. "I believe you, all right. But I have trouble picturing an education that includes sword fighting but no cooking lessons."

"That's because you're not royal."

She hadn't meant it critically, but he took it that way, she saw, when his face became set. Despair welled up. Every time they started to erode the barriers of class and country that separated them, she inadvertently said or did something to replace them.

It was his fault. If he would allow her to forget her position for one minute, she wouldn't keep reminding him. But he kept provoking the reminders, as if he was in some danger of forgetting. When he kissed her, he *had* forgotten, she would swear. So had she, but she refused to think about it now, when Hugh was standing close enough to touch.

She tossed the poker down, and it landed on the hearth with a clang like the closing of a prison door. Touching him was the last thing she should do. It was bad enough that he threatened every dream she owned. Now he made her long for things she had no business wanting.

A real home, children, normalcy. The power of the yearnings caught her off guard as the thought of bearing Hugh's children fisted a huge lump of need inside her. She told herself it was this crazy situation, making everything seem more intimate. Making her see what she needed to see in Hugh.

Tomorrow everything would look different.

She controlled her voice with an effort. "What about the bed?"

"We'll try that your way, too."

Her heart sank. *Now* he was ready to share the bed with her. Why couldn't he have given in while she was good and mad at him, instead of waiting until she was a quivering mass of longing and sensations.

"Do you prefer to sleep on the outside or against the wall?"

She affected a shrug to hide her inner turmoil. "Up to you."

"Maybe I'd better take the wall."

He didn't want her to feel trapped, she gathered. She nodded. "Thank you."

Kicking off his boots, he arranged two pillows at the end of the mattress closest to the fire, then stretched full-length on the platform, tugging two of the blankets over himself. He held one corner open. "Coming?"

"I'm not tired yet," she lied.

"Suit yourself. Tomorrow is another long day."

Today already qualified, she thought. The ride and the long walk to the cabin had exhausted her. She longed for sleep. But she couldn't bring herself to lie down beside Hugh. In accusing him of being unable to control himself, she was afraid she had been speaking for herself.

For the next half hour she remained stiffly upright on one of the uncomfortable wooden chairs, watching the fire die down slowly. When the chill began to seep into her bones, she knew she couldn't delay any longer. Hugh's breathing had slowed. He was asleep. She decided it was as safe as it would ever be to risk joining him.

Careful not to disturb him, she slid her boots off and climbed into the makeshift bed. It had looked wider than it was, or else she hadn't allowed for Hugh's size. She froze as her hip connected with his. She held her breath but he didn't stir.

Telling herself she was glad he was asleep didn't stop an aching sense of need from sweeping through her. She didn't want him to be asleep. She wanted him to open heavy-lidded eyes and see her, then open his arms and enfold her. She was certifiably crazy.

As the only girl among her siblings, she had often been alone but had never felt lonely before. The sprawling palaces and the country villa she had occupied in solitary splendor had never felt empty until she met Hugh.

Now the thought of sharing all those halls and galleries, staterooms and gardens with no one but her retinue of staff held a lot less appeal. She wanted someone there for her, she realized. Someone to share her breakfast before starting the day. Someone to talk things over with after a day filled with official engagements. Someone whose arms would shelter her during sleep.

Someone to love her.

She knew the someone wasn't Hugh. He didn't want her or her life-style. It was small comfort that he had admitted he found her attractive, but he plainly intended to do nothing about it.

If he won the challenge, he would take Carazzan and set up his ranch, and she would see him only in her official capacity. If she won, he would probably leave Carramer and be equally lost to her.

She knew she should welcome them, but neither prospect held very much appeal.

He rolled over in his sleep, bringing his hard body into closer alignment with hers. Gingerly she turned on her side, trying to still the fast beating of her heart. It didn't work. As long as any part of him touched her, her imagination kept lurching into overdrive. Slowly she eased herself to the very edge of the platform and drew the meager covering tighter around herself.

It helped for a time, and she was able to drift into a fitful sleep. When she awoke with a start, trying to get her bearings, she found that the fire had almost gone out. She was freezing.

With a sigh of resignation she made herself relax against Hugh, feeling the warmth of his body drive out some of the chill, as he could drive out her loneliness if they weren't so ill-matched. It was a foolish hope, but she felt comforted by it as she went back to sleep.

Hugh awoke first and wondered why he had no feeling in his left arm. Then he saw the reason, and tension rippled through him, followed almost instantly by a powerful sense of arousal he had no business feeling. Not with this woman.

While she slept she had snuggled against him and now lay in the crook of his arm, her lithe body neatly aligned with his. In sleep, he had thrown one leg over hers, and the intimacy of it took his breath away. He had only to turn his head slightly to bring her delicious mouth within kissing distance.

He knew immediately that he wouldn't be able to stop at kissing. Lord, how he wanted her. Right now, with her glorious black hair spilling across his chest and her limbs entwined with his, he wanted everything she was capable of giving. And he knew instinctively that it would be a lot.

Why couldn't she have been an ordinary woman, the Dee he'd met at the fair? Then they could enjoy each other without strings, without anybody getting hurt. He wasn't the right man for a princess. He was self-made and self-centered, and content to be both.

With grim humor he remembered the quote about the self-made man having a fool for a maker. In this case it was true, at least where Adrienne was concerned.

He lay in agony, mental and physical. He couldn't get up without disturbing her. And he had to get up or he wouldn't answer for the consequences. As carefully as he could, he brushed her lips with his. It took a lot not to follow his instincts and deepen the kiss.

Her long lashes fluttered, and she looked at him, sleep confusing her senses. She looked impossibly young and beautiful. "What are you doing?"

He managed a taut smile. "Waking you in the traditional way."

He saw the moment when she awoke fully. The doe-eyed creature in his arms vanished as the princess reasserted herself. He had to admire the dignified way she unwound herself from him, but wished she would hurry it up. This slow disentangling of limbs did nothing to lessen his arousal.

By the time she was back on her side of the bed, hot, pulsating need pounded through him. By sheer force of will he controlled it and slid past her, dropping to the cold, bare floor. He let the chill seep up his legs as the next best thing to a cold shower. Then he sat on one of the straight-backed chairs to pull his boots on.

Adrienne watched him warily. She sensed his tension and could guess the reason for it. She felt her face flame as she thought of how she had curled herself around him in sleep. It wasn't intentional, she had been trying to get warm, but it meant she couldn't ignore her effect on him this morning.

Why hadn't he taken advantage? The answer was as swift as it was unflattering. He still didn't want to. At some level had she hoped to drive him to a frenzy of wanting her, so she could then refuse him? It seemed possible.

Playing games with a man like Hugh was not only unworthy, it was dangerous, she told herself. What would she have done if he *had* decided to make the most of their situation? She should be glad his strength had prevailed. She wasn't.

What did she want from him? She tried to tell herself it was the land for her dream ranch, but suspected it was no longer the whole answer. What she wanted from him was so wrong, she hardly dared put it into words.

"Staying in bed all day?" he asked in a grating voice.

He had built up the fire again and placed a saucepan of water on it. As she watched him spoon instant coffee into plastic cups, she felt her heart squeeze as if in a vise. The morning beard darkening his jaw made him look rugged, almost piratical and his hair was mussed where he'd run his fingers through it instead of a comb.

His shirt was unbuttoned almost to the waist and she glimpsed rippling muscles lightly dusted with dark hair. Primal need slammed through her. She ached to call him back to bed, to finish what his touch had started.

Resolutely she thrust the blankets aside and got out, wishing she didn't look and feel so crumpled. He poured boiling water into the cups and handed one to her. "It probably isn't what you're used to, but it's the best the kitchen can do."

Aromatic stream curled around her face. "It smells wonderful."

So did she, he thought. He half-drained his cup and stood up. "You can use the sink to freshen up. I'll go see to the horses."

He couldn't wait to get away from her, she thought, anger rising. "Don't you need to shave?"

"With what? I'm sorry if I offend your royal sensibility, but I didn't come prepared to stay out all night."

"You don't offend me. I was thinking of you."

She thought she heard him mutter something about a first time for everything, then he barreled out of the hut. By the time he returned she had washed in the freezing water and wrestled open a can of beans for their breakfast. This time she made sure it didn't catch fire.

Hugh wasted little time cleaning his plate, then started gathering their things. He plainly couldn't wait to get back to the challenge. Instead of being glad, she felt as cheated as a bride on her wedding night, whose husband chose to watch television instead of spending time with her.

Fool, she told herself. This was hardly a honeymoon suite, and Hugh couldn't have made his indifference much more obvious. Resignedly she took the plates to the sink and washed them.

Less than half an hour later the cabin was tidy and ready for anyone else needing shelter for the night. The horses were fresh and eager to be off. Adrienne wished she could say the same for herself.

Chapter Nine

After the violence of last night's storm, the rain-drenched forest smelled sweet and fresh and the sky was so blue it hurt her eyes. Brushing an overhanging branch brought raindrops scattering over her face and down the back of her neck. Few other signs of the storm's fury remained, other than a tangle of trees that had come down during the night.

Guiding Gypsy carefully around them, Adrienne was glad they hadn't tried to go any farther than the cabin. The mud, potholes and fallen leaves made the going bad enough in broad daylight. In failing light it would have been suicidal.

Hugh had allowed her to start ahead of him, but she doubted he was being gallant. In the sea of mud that the storm had made of the trail, Avatar was much more sure-footed than Gypsy, as Hugh would have discovered yesterday. Any head start he gave her would be eaten up by his faster progress within a short time.

For the first time she faced the possibility of losing the challenge. Unfortunately, Hugh was right, she was a

woman of her word. If he won, she would relinquish Carazzan, and the dreams that went with him, to Hugh. Bad
enough to lose so much, but how could she accept never
again going out as Dee?

A dripping branch slapped her in the face, and she
snapped out of it, berating herself for thinking of the contest
as lost already. The day was far from over. Gypsy might
not be as surefooted as Avatar in these conditions, but the
mare had courage and determination. So did Adrienne.
They weren't beaten yet.

She heard the drum of hooves behind her and urged
Gypsy on. There had to be a way to reach the ranger station
at the foot of the mountain before Hugh did.

There was.

She had been letting herself think of this trail as the only
way. After the storm it was the only *safe* way. But the rules
of the Nuee Challenge were clear. A rider could take any
route as long as they collected a marker from the summit
and delivered it to the ranger station at the foot of the
mountain where the time and the code on it would be
logged as proof of their achievement.

Before she could give herself time to change her mind,
she pulled on the reins, causing Gypsy to swerve into the
forest. The going would be rough, perhaps rougher than the
official endurance route they had followed yesterday, but it
would be faster than sticking to the tourist trail.

Hugh might have the same idea, of course. But he didn't
know this country as well as she did. She might not have
ridden the Nuee Challenge, but she had spent plenty of time
exploring Nuee's forests under all conditions.

Perhaps not as bad as this, she admitted. Her brothers
would go crazy if they saw her skidding down the muddy
inclines, her fingers tangled in Gypsy's mane for extra pur-
chase.

Hooves churned through water as she crossed a creek swollen with rain. She let Gypsy drop her head and drink, then she dismounted and used her hands to splash the sweat away from her horse's steaming flanks.

She ate an apple from her pack but stopped only long enough to be sure she wasn't overtaxing Gypsy. Time was her enemy now, time and the man somewhere on the mountain, ahead or behind her—she no longer had any idea. Suddenly the sound of hooves brought her head around.

He couldn't.

But he had. Somehow Hugh had followed her through the trackless forest. She stared in helpless fury as he rode past, waving a greeting as he went.

Of all the…she slapped her hat into the water in anger. She couldn't help leaving a trail, but she hadn't expected Hugh to follow it or her. The advantage she had hoped to gain by striking out on her own was suddenly lost.

That meant war. She rammed the hat into her saddlebag and swung herself into the saddle. "Female honor is at stake," she told Gypsy. "You can't let me down now."

The plucky horse didn't. She delivered everything Adrienne asked of her and more, keeping her footing over mud-soaked leaves and fallen logs, climbing ridges and plunging into valleys like the champion she was.

Adrienne felt the adrenaline rush of the most exciting ride she had ever tackled. Whatever the outcome, she knew she would remember this for a long, long time.

Then the wild stallion appeared in her path.

Out of nowhere, he was suddenly *there,* breathtakingly beautiful with dark eyes, white mane and a coat of pure gold. She dragged in a stunned breath. He could have been Carazzan's cousin. Carazzan didn't have a white mane. But in perfection of line and beauty of confirmation, and in every other way she knew to judge a horse, he was second only to her magnificent Carazzan.

Gypsy blew air through her nostrils and skittered sideways. The wild stallion, one of the wonderful native horses that roamed these forests, suddenly reared up.

Gypsy responded by rearing, too, and flailing her head around. With all her skill, Adrienne found she could barely hold her. What was the matter with her? Then it dawned on her. It was almost spring. Gypsy must be coming into season. She was reacting as any red-blooded female would when confronted with a perfect specimen of the opposite sex.

Normally Adrienne would have noticed and chosen another horse for the challenge. But Hugh had distracted her so much that she had overlooked the signs. And Gypsy hadn't reacted to Avatar because the other horse was a gelding.

"Easy, girl, easy," she urged, struggling to control the lunging horse. Suddenly Gypsy gave a violent buck that tore the reins out of Adrienne's hands. She flew through the air.

Landing heavily, she cried out as her foot caught on a tree root, sending a wrenching pain all the way to her thigh.

"Stay there, don't try to stand."

Where had Hugh come from? He must have heard the squealing horses and come back to investigate. Without hesitation, he rode between Gypsy and the stallion, waving his hat and yelling at the wild horse. With a high-pitched neigh, the stallion wheeled away into the forest.

Gypsy came to a standstill, looking around as if she wasn't sure what had just happened. Before the mare could follow the stallion into the forest, Hugh grabbed her reins and led her back to Adrienne. He tied both horses to a tree and dropped down beside her. "Are you all right?"

"I'm fine, thanks."

"I heard you cry out. Is it your ankle?"

If he knew she was hurt, he would insist on ending the contest. She hadn't come this far to give up now, although she had a suspicion the accident had aggravated the ankle she had damaged as a teenager. "I twisted it, nothing serious."

To demonstrate, she put her weight onto both feet. The pain almost finished her, but she pasted a smile onto her face. "No real harm done."

His suspicious look raked her. "Are you able to ride?"

She would ride if it killed her. "As long as Gypsy behaves herself."

There was no need to explain. Hugh had sized up the situation at once. "She should be all right, provided you don't meet any more equine Don Juans."

"Then what are we waiting for?"

He was waiting to see her mount Gypsy, she guessed. She managed to maneuver the horse around so she could mount on the side away from Hugh. It was a lip-biting, white-knuckle experience, but she made it into the saddle.

He still looked skeptical. There was only one solution. Careful of her damaged ankle, she urged Gypsy into action, aiming her at a break in the trees. As if ashamed of letting her mistress down before, the mare took off like a rocket, carrying Adrienne past a startled Hugh and into the forest.

She managed to hold the lead for the rest of the descent until the forest gave way to level ground. From here it was a gallop across open country to the ranger station. Exhilaration made the pain bearable. She was going to do it. She was going to win.

But before she had covered more than half the distance, Hugh pulled into the clearing and came after her at a pace she knew Gypsy couldn't match. It didn't stop the mare from sensing a race and going flat-out as soon as Adrienne gave her full rein. From the corner of her eye, Adrienne saw Hugh gaining on her.

Pain throbbed through her ankle with every thundering stride the mare took. She gritted her teeth, managing to hold her own until Avatar wheeled in close to Gypsy. As they rode neck and neck, Hugh's boot accidentally bumped her damaged foot in the stirrup. The brief contact was enough to drag a cry of pain from her. She swayed and would have fallen again if he hadn't reached across and steadied her with one strong arm.

As he reined in Avatar, Gypsy slowed, too, both horses coming to a stop within sight of the ranger station. Hugh was out of the saddle in time to catch her as she fell. She felt as though in a dream as his arms closed around her, wondering if his lips really did graze her forehead, or was it a product of her fevered imagination? Then everything went black.

She came to on a couch in the ranger's office. The ranger looked as if he couldn't do enough to please Hugh, who barked out orders as if he was the one with the title. They knew who she was, she saw in dismay as her head cleared, recognizing the fuss that her presence inevitably caused. Had Hugh given her away? He didn't have to, she realized, remembering the hat and the sunglasses in her saddlebag. She struggled upright.

Hugh was at her side at once. "Take it easy, Your Highness. Your helicopter's on the way. A doctor is standing by."

"I don't need a doctor. I'm fine."

"I can see that. Lie still and be happy you're still in one piece."

In a manner of speaking, she thought, unable to deny

that it felt good to have Hugh fussing over her. Better than berating her, anyway. Her eyes started to drift shut, and she forced them open on a sudden suspicion.

It was confirmed when she saw a dirt-streaked jade marker lying on the ranger's desk. She might have known Hugh would make sure his victory was recorded, even while taking care of her.

He had won after all. She'd half expected it, but the pain was almost as acute as the one in her ankle. Carazzan, the land, her freedom, Hugh—all gone because of one stupid accident.

She tried to track the pain to its source. The stallion had shown her that there were other horses of Carazzan's caliber. The land was never hers to begin with. And her freedom was illusory at best. So why did she feel as if her world had come to an end?

Hugh. The truth that had started to dawn during the troubled night could no longer be denied. She was in love with him. For all the good it would do her. He didn't want her. He definitely didn't love her. Now that he had what he wanted, she would be lucky ever to see him again.

The helicopter ride passed in a haze of vibration that jarred her ankle until she had to clench her teeth to keep silent. She was mildly surprised that Hugh traveled with her and stayed at her side through a blur of X-rays, pain-killing injections and lectures from her doctor about fools and horses.

"That doctor was pretty rough on you," Hugh said when they were left alone briefly.

She managed a weak smile. "Alain Pascale delivered all the royal babies including me. It makes him proprietary. But he cares a lot and he's gentle when it counts."

Hugh was angry for her sake, she thought on a swell of pride. He cared at least that much. Knowing he would soon be gone made it all the more precious. "Dr. Pascale says I can go home now, provided I agree to rest."

"Maybe you should stay here overnight."

"The doctor suggested it, but I refused." She caught something odd in Hugh's manner. "Is there a reason why I shouldn't go home?"

"About a dozen reasons, all of them paparazzi and all of them camped outside the hospital, waiting for you to appear."

Her eyes went wide. "Because of the accident?"

"No, because of this." He held out the day's copy of the Carramer *Independent*. Most of the front page was taken up by a photograph of Adrienne disguised as Dee. Hugh had his arm around her.

She recognized the location as the members' pavilion at the showground. "It must have been taken when you took me for coffee after..."

He nodded. "I didn't know then why you were so anxious not to be noticed by the photographers taking pictures of the Show Princess. One of them must have snapped this when you tried to leave, when you stumbled and I steadied you."

It looked much more damning, she thought, like a secret tryst. She was almost afraid to read the rest but made herself scan it. "It's all here, your visit to my villa, even the fact that we spent last night together on the mountain. How could they know so much?"

"One of your trusted staff."

"They wouldn't."

"They would. It happened to me after my wife left. She planted rumors about my finances that one of my staff was happy to verify for money. Most of them were loyal, but it only takes one bad apple."

"What are we going to do?"

He ticked off steps on one hand. "First get you home, then work out a cover story that gets you off the hook."

And himself, she thought painfully. Now that the land and Carazzan were secure, he wouldn't want a scandal jeopardizing his business interests.

Being royal had some benefits, she thought. When they explained the situation, Dr. Pascale arranged for a decoy group to leave by the main entrance of the hospital while Hugh wheeled her out of a side door and into a waiting limousine.

This time she was grateful for the presence of her bodyguard and driver. Being alone with Hugh, knowing that he didn't return her feelings, would hurt worse than her injury.

But it wasn't over yet. She had been home for only long enough to freshen up and change when Cindy told her, "Prince Lorne is on the phone for you." Her expression warned Adrienne that her brother wasn't calling about her health.

Adrienne lay on a chaise longue with a blanket over her legs. Her assistant put the call through on the speaker before leaving the room. Lorne wasted no time on pleasantries. "What in the name of heaven do you think you're doing?"

She made a face at Hugh. "I'm feeling much better, thank you. My ankle was only sprained and needs rest."

Normally Lorne would have heard the hurt in her voice and relented a little. This time he ignored it. "So Alain tells me, and I'm relieved to hear it. The doctor also tells me you wouldn't have been injured if you hadn't behaved so recklessly. For goodness' sake! There's already a minority faction calling for Carramer to be made a republic. They're regarded as a joke, but for how much longer if you give them so much ammunition?"

She sobered. "None of this was supposed to be made public."

"None of what?" Lorne asked. She sensed that he was hoping for a less damning explanation than the story in the paper.

Hugh surprised her by stepping closer to the speaker. "Your Highness, forgive the intrusion. I'm Hugh Jordan and I can explain what this is all about."

"Michel spoke highly of the work you're doing together," the ruler commented, his voice hard. "But that was before you were photographed with Adrienne."

"I understand, sir, but you should know that I'm in love with the princess."

Adrienne's indrawn breath carried down the speaker to Lorne as Hugh added, "We intended to wait until the princess had spoken with you, but after what's happened, there's no point keeping our feelings to ourselves any longer. I regret not being able to do this in person, but I want to ask your blessing to marry Princess Adrienne."

Adrienne swallowed hard. Knowing how much she wished Hugh was sincere, she found his announcement overwhelming. The ruler gave her no time for reflection, and she heard the controlled anger in his voice as he said, "Are you in love with Hugh, Adrienne?"

She might be guilty of keeping some activities to herself, but she wasn't in the habit of lying to her brother and was glad she could be honest now. "Yes, I am."

"This is rather sudden, isn't it?"

Again, Hugh spoke first. "Love doesn't work to a timetable, sir. Sometimes it happens against all common sense."

"As on this occasion," Lorne agreed coldly. Adrienne braced herself for her brother's lecture on the unsuitability of Hugh as a consort. He had every right. Hugh was wrong for her in every way that mattered except one—the way she felt about him.

She couldn't allow Lorne to demean Hugh in any way, so she said quickly, "I'm sure you remember what it was like for you and Alison."

There was a long silence, then Lorne said heavily, "Fortunately for you I do, but at least we had the sense to be more discreet."

"I'm sorry about that," she conceded. "I should have realized what might happen."

"Regrets won't remedy the situation," Lorne pointed out. "But there is something that might."

"What do you suggest?"

"We let it be known that your sojourn on the mountain amounted to a Wedding Eve."

Quickly she explained to Hugh about the Carramer custom where engaged couples spent a night together in celibate seclusion as part of their wedding preparations. She hadn't thought of the night at the cabin that way, but it fitted perfectly. All that was missing was the wedding intention itself, and she couldn't let herself think about that now. She lifted her head. "Hugh?"

He nodded. "I'm willing."

Lorne was already moving on. "Good. There will still be talk, but it will be far less damaging to Adrienne and the family. Naturally, I would have preferred you both to discuss this with me before your relationship became public knowledge, but we must deal with the situation as it exists."

"Thank you, sir. We appreciate your understanding."

"Don't thank me yet. My dear sister will be a challenge, I promise."

"Lorne, please."

Hugh didn't look at her. "I know and I think I can cope."

"Be sure of it, Hugh. In Carramer, marriage is a lifetime commitment."

She studied Hugh under lowered lashes, but the news didn't seem to trouble him, probably because he knew it wouldn't come to a real marriage. "I'm aware of it, Your Highness," he said.

"Then I look forward to meeting you officially, Hugh. In the meantime the palace will announce your engagement and ask for you to be given privacy while Adrienne recovers from her injury. As soon as you're well enough, we'll make plans to introduce Hugh to the people."

By then they would have fallen out of 'love' as quickly as they fell into it, she thought, unable to subdue a flash of misery. Hugh had invented the engagement to protect her reputation, not because he shared her feelings. "Yes, Lorne," she told her brother, dejection keeping her tone low.

Lorne's voice softened. "And next time, Adrienne, it might help to talk to me before doing anything so rash."

"I will."

When Lorne rang off, Hugh gave her an odd look. "It seems we're engaged."

She twisted her hands together and nodded, feeling oddly shy suddenly. "Thank you for covering for me."

"My pleasure, princess." He knelt beside her couch and took her face in both hands, planting a deep, satisfying kiss on her half-open mouth.

Emotions whirled through her, too fast to catalog, too sweet to endure. When he pulled away, her eyes were moist. He frowned. "What's this? I was only sealing our bargain."

"It isn't every day that a woman gets engaged," she said

in an attempt to cover her discomfiture. The passion in his kiss reminded her how much she wished it could be genuine.

Before she could say more, he stood abruptly and strode to the door, wrenching it open. Cindy was on the threshold, obviously listening. He grabbed the woman's hand and pulled her inside, closing the door again. High spots of red color stood out on Cindy's cheeks.

"Care to explain?" he demanded.

Cindy glanced uncertainly at Adrienne. "What does he mean, Your Highness?"

Hugh answered for her. "I think you know. You're the one who betrayed the princess to the press, aren't you? Were you listening for more juicy tidbits to pass on to them?"

"I wasn't...I didn't."

"Did you go to the press, Cindy?" Adrienne asked quietly, her tone vibrant with disappointment. Somehow she knew what the woman's answer would be.

Cindy buried her face in her hands. "Yes. I'm so sorry. I'd give anything to undo it."

"Why, Cindy? I trusted you."

Cindy avoided Adrienne's eyes. "Two weeks ago when you borrowed my car and went out as Dee, I decided to pretend I was you. I was at a window wearing one of your gowns and a tiara when Sam Joffe, that awful photographer from the Independent, snapped me with a long lens. In the city next day he showed me the picture and threatened to publish it if I didn't agree to be his...source, he called it."

"Spy is a better word," Hugh said coldly.

He was probably furious because Cindy's actions had forced him into pretending to be engaged to her, Adrienne thought unhappily. "So you told him where I went and what I did."

"Nothing they couldn't have found out for themselves, I swear. I didn't alert them when you went to the show."

Hugh stepped forward. "Then how did he get that picture of the two of us together?"

"Sam Joffe was there with the press contingent, photographing Miss Show Princess," Adrienne reminded him.

"And he got lucky," Hugh concluded heavily. "It doesn't explain how they knew where we were last night."

Cindy looked wretched. "I told them that. They planned to run the picture of the two of you and wanted more details. Who Mr. Jordan was, and what his connection with the princess. I was so jealous of you, Your Highness. And so mad at you. You had everything I wanted and you didn't seem to want it."

Her shy glance at Hugh told its own story. A pang shot through Adrienne as she realized that her assistant was attracted to the rugged American. How much better suited they would be than she and Hugh. At the same time, a feeling so savagely primitive shot through her that she was shocked. Enduring Cindy's betrayal was somehow easier than thinking of her with the man Adrienne herself loved.

She couldn't bear to imagine any other woman in his arms, she thought.

Cindy shifted from one foot to the other. "My resignation will be on your desk as soon as I've packed. I'll be gone by tonight."

"Not so fast," Adrienne said. The other woman looked startled. "The Right to Ride organization is looking for a full-time secretary. I won't conceal from them the reason you're leaving, but in light of your otherwise exemplary record, I'm sure they would consider you for the job."

Cindy looked disbelieving. "You'd help me get another job, after what I did?"

"You've been a perfect aide for three years. I've asked

a lot of you lately, perhaps more than I had a right to. I can't excuse your behavior, but I can understand it a little.'' Hugh had also accused Adrienne of not appreciating what she had. She was beginning to wonder if they were right. She might not regret seeing the last of Dee after all.

Cindy smiled her relief. ''Nothing like this will ever happen again, I swear.''

Somehow Adrienne knew that Cindy meant what she said. She dismissed the woman, who left with alacrity. Hugh turned to her. ''It's tough having your trust betrayed, isn't it?''

''Voice of experience, Hugh?''

''I told you what I went through after my marriage ended. Don't let it stop you from trusting again.''

She turned her head away. ''How can I have trust, after what just happened?''

He sat alongside her on the couch and took her hand. ''How would you rehabilitate a horse that had lost its trust in people?''

Heat from his hand traveled along her arm. Emotion clogged her throat as she looked at him. ''With kindness and love.''

He lifted her hand and rubbed it along the side of his face. Like her, he had showered and changed as soon as they returned to the villa, and his newly shaved face felt like velvet under her hand. ''Then treat yourself the same. Don't blame yourself for not suspecting Cindy.''

''You did,'' she pointed out, recalling his warning at the cabin.

''As you told me yourself, I'm not royal.''

This time there was no resentment in his tone. He was simply reminding her of reality. So she wouldn't read too much into their pretend engagement? It seemed likely. She wished she had the will to pull her hand out of his and send him away so she could give in to the tears hovering behind her eyes.

Instead, she curled her fingers into his palm, drawing comfort from the strength that flowed from him to her. He wasn't royal but he had foreseen Cindy's problem before Adrienne herself had. "I won't mind not being Dee anymore," she said in a low voice. "She's served her purpose."

"And the ranch?"

"It's yours," she said simply. "It always was. I was a fool to think a princess could walk away from everything and be an ordinary person."

"You could never be ordinary."

"Don't humor me," she said, her tone brittle to the point of nearly breaking.

His eyebrows canted upward. "What makes you think I'm humoring you? You're a special person, Adrienne, not just because of your title, but because of who you are inside. I got to know that person pretty well over the past couple of days."

Picturing herself tired, covered in mud, she was forced to laugh. "And you can still pay me compliments?"

He smiled, evidently sharing the memory. "It isn't difficult. What I saw out there was a woman of extraordinary beauty, courage and determination. She can do anything she sets her mind to."

Except the one thing she wanted, make Hugh love her, she admitted to herself. She should be comforted to have reached some kind of détente with him, but instead she felt as if the gulf between them was wider than ever.

She almost preferred him to be mad at her, she realized. At least then she had something to fight. Having him be kind to her threatened her self-control too much.

"What will you do now?" she asked, finding it hard to

say the words when she knew what his answer was likely
to be.

She was wrong. "I'll come to see you every day until
you're fully recovered. Your Dr. Pascale tells me it could
be a week or more."

The thought of having him at her side for another week
filled her with elation, although it would make the inevi-
table parting that much harder. It was only for appearances'
sake, she knew, not because he wanted to stay with her.
"Don't you have meetings with Michel on Isle des Anges?"

"I can fly there and back in a day."

She fiddled with a corner of the blanket. "Why are you
doing this?"

"Doing what?"

"You didn't have to pretend we were engaged. You
could have let me deal with the problem on my own. As
Lorne pointed out, I got myself into it."

Hugh uncoiled from the couch and strode to the window,
looking out for a moment before turning back to her. "Is
it so hard to accept that I might want to do you a favor."

So she would owe him one in return when he finally
established his ranch? She didn't like to think so, but it
seemed possible. Favors had been the currency of royalty
around the world for centuries. Why should things be different in Carramer? He hadn't said the engagement was
what he wanted, she noticed. No surprises there.

"I'd like to rest now," she said formally.

"Then I'll see you at dinner."

The image this conjured up was so cozily domestic that
she rejected it instinctively. They might be engaged in the
eyes of the world, but she had better not start thinking of
the engagement as genuine. She was at risk of doing so
because she wanted so much for it to be real. The breath

caught in her throat, and she made herself say, "I'm sure you'd rather return to your hotel so I'll have something sent to my room."

His expression turned cold as he recognized the dismissal for what it was. "As you wish, Your Highness."

She couldn't let him leave in such an angry mood, although she wasn't sure what he had to be angry about. She was only facing facts. "Hugh?"

Halfway to the door he froze in midstride. "Yes?"

"Since we're engaged to be married, shouldn't you call me Adrienne?"

"As you wish, Your Highness."

The door closed behind him. She let out a shuddering sigh but refused to give in to the tears hovering a heartbeat away. She should be glad that Hugh had retreated from her again. In theory she should find it easier to endure the week or so he had elected to remain nearby to give their supposed engagement more credibility.

He had called her beautiful, courageous and determined, but it wasn't enough to make him love her. And this time all the power at her command couldn't change a thing. What was the good of being royal when it couldn't give you your heart's desire, she asked herself bitterly.

Then she drew herself up. If Hugh wanted royal, she would give him royal. She had a week to rebuild her defences against him. A week to turn back into the princess she had tried to escape being, as Hugh and Cindy had rightly chastised her over. Then she would tackle her duties with a new fervor that would please even her brothers.

No one would be allowed to suspect what Hugh had come to mean to her, she resolved, especially not Hugh himself. Not by a word or glance would she betray her love for him, no matter what the cost, and she suspected it would be considerable. Her heart, her future? All of the above? She refused to think about it now.

He didn't want her? So be it. She had a kingdom for consolation. It would be enough because it had to be.

Chapter Ten

Getting back to his hotel was a gauntlet Hugh hadn't prepared himself to run, and the experience didn't help his mood in the least. He was reminded too much of the turmoil he'd endured after Jemima had left.

Without consulting him, Adrienne had assigned a minder to go with him, although Hugh had assured the man that he could take care of himself. Now he was glad of the help to bulldoze through the clamoring media to get to his room where the minder stationed himself outside Hugh's door.

Staying at the royal villa would have avoided this circus, but he needed time alone to think. Besides, Adrienne had made it clear she didn't want him to stay, he thought grimly.

His sudden notoriety had improved the service, he noted. Scotch? Of course, sir. The best we have. On the house. Delivered in the blink of an eye. Was there anything else he needed, anything at all? He had only to ask. Good grief, how did Adrienne put up with this on a daily basis?

Thinking of her, he felt his features soften, and he drew

in air as he remembered the feel of her mouth against his. Better not think of that. He had called her courageous without telling her how much he admired the way she'd finished the ride, injured ankle and all. Not many women he knew would have done it.

He wanted to wring her beautiful neck, of course. The ankle could have been broken. She had injured it years before, so it was probably weakened. She could have fallen off Gypsy and been killed. During the final reckless gallop, she had been out of his sight for minutes at a time. If he hadn't been there to catch her when she fell...

He put the drink aside and dropped to a chair, resting his head in his hands, as he imagined finding her lifeless body slumped on the forest floor. Cold sweat broke out on his forehead, and when he held his hands in front of him, they shook.

When had he started caring so much? When he woke up beside her in the cabin, he decided. Feeling her supple body coiled against him had stirred more than his hormones. It had stirred something a lot deeper, something he had been trying to avoid facing. Love? He didn't know what to call it, but he knew it made him want to wake up beside her every day for the rest of his life.

With her stunning looks, it wasn't hard to imagine the beautiful babies they could make together. He found himself grinning. What if they ended up with his looks? Then he sobered. It wasn't going to happen. The fiction of an engagement was to protect her reputation, not because it was possible.

When he had suggested having dinner with her, she had been quick enough to remind him of his place, he noted. Happy to use him as Jemima had done and then wash her hands of him.

No, not like Jemima. Nothing about Adrienne was like

his ex-wife, he thought. Adrienne was not a user. She had been shocked when he'd told her brother they were engaged, he remembered. She had been prepared to face the consequences of her actions. He was the one who had wanted to protect her. There was something else she said, too. When Prince Lorne asked her if she loved Hugh, she had said yes.

She might avoid telling the whole truth, but she wasn't a liar, either.

His heart picked up speed. Could she possibly feel for him some of what he felt for her? He retrieved the scotch and downed half of it in one swallow. What did it matter? Whether she loved him or not, she was still the princess.

They were too different in background and life-styles. Coming from nowhere, he was driven to make something of himself. She was born to status and wealth. As the physical attraction between them inevitably mellowed, what would replace it? He couldn't see himself as her handbag, decorating her arm when she did her princess thing.

How long before she turned to a more willing escort who fitted her life-style better than Hugh did? He almost crushed the glass in nerveless fingers, but made himself face reality. Hell would turn into the cubes in this drink before a relationship between them stood a chance of working.

"How's the patient today?"

Adrienne looked up from the thank-you notes she was signing in response to the mountain of best wishes the announcement of her engagement had generated to find Michel standing beside her. She put the paperwork aside and opened her arms for a hug from her tall, handsome brother.

"Getting impatient," she said when he straightened.

"But it's heaven to be walking on two feet again after a week of being wrapped in cotton wool."

Michel dragged a chaise longue closer to Adrienne's under an umbrella beside the shimmering pool and sat down. "I hope you aren't rushing things."

She pushed her sunglasses onto the top of her head. "Dr. Pascale assures me I'm not."

His gesture took in the pile of correspondence. "I didn't mean the ankle. I meant this engagement of yours."

She felt herself color. "I suppose you agree with Lorne that I'm crazy."

"We all have our own kinds of craziness, Lorne included. Everything was stacked against him and Alison, but look how happy they are now."

"Was it like that when you met Caroline?"

The prince nodded. "Her having an identical twin complicated things, but I never doubted which twin I loved."

"Did she love you?"

His expression softened. "It took me a while to realize how much."

"How did you finally figure it out?"

He smiled. "She told me, not in so many words, but by her actions. The point is, Lorne and I nearly let love slip through our fingers. I'm glad you've learned from our mistakes."

She made a face. "It's about the only benefit of being the youngest."

He looked thoughtful. "Don't blame us for wanting to protect you, Adrienne. If our parents had lived, things may have been different. Their deaths reminded us how fragile life is and how important we are to each other."

She touched his hand lightly. "I know. I'm accused of not appreciating my family, but I do, more than I can say."

"We've never doubted it."

He looked at his watch. "I must go, but I'll be back to have lunch with you. Originally I intended to meet Hugh on Anges, but I wanted to see you, so I suggested we meet here. I hope it isn't inconvenient?" She shook her head, and Michel paused. "If he is the man for you, I want you to know you have my blessing. Lorne's, too."

"Thanks, big brother." The words came out choked. It meant a lot to have both her brothers' approval, even if it was misplaced. In the week since the challenge, Hugh had become noticeably cooler toward her. He only visited her at the villa each day to keep up the fiction that they were engaged, she guessed.

She had learned from him that his plans for the new ranch were nearly final. So it wouldn't be long before he called an end to the engagement. She wasn't looking forward to making new headlines, but living without Hugh would be harder by far.

She should be glad the deception had served its purpose, deflecting public attention from Dee and the night she and Hugh had spent together on the mountain, but she couldn't feel grateful when it was tearing her apart inside.

She imagined the meeting between Hugh and Michel at that moment. Would Hugh bring up Carazzan's role in his breeding program? He hadn't yet claimed the horse, but he had told her of visiting the land. Work had already commenced on the new facilities, so Carazzan would be there before long.

Hugh would soon be there.

She accepted that losing Carazzan, hard though it might be, wasn't what bothered her. It was the thought of Hugh living so close, but as unreachable as the moon, that was like a knife twisting inside her.

This would have to stop. Her foot was almost better. Time she picked herself up and got on with her life.

Matching thoughts with action, she stood, relieved to feel hardly a twinge in her damaged ankle. The pain around her heart was another matter, but she ignored it and set off for the stable. She would have to say goodbye to Carazzan, and now was as good a time as any.

The staff looked surprised to see her. She greeted them distantly and made for Carazzan's stable. But his stall was empty.

None of the staff she accosted could explain where Carazzan had gone. The groom who had taken him out for his morning exercise had reported no problems, she was told, but she was assured that a search would be started at once. Carazzan would be located.

She didn't think they would have far to look. Anger began to burn inside her, hot and violent. Hugh had the right, but she hadn't expected him to take the horse without doing her the courtesy of warning her. It was too much.

She wheeled around and stormed back inside, finding Hugh in the study, poring over sheafs of papers. Michel had gone. "Should you be walking around?" Hugh asked.

Her gaze flashed fire at him. "You'd prefer it if I didn't, I suppose."

"Only for your sake."

"Not because having me up and about interferes with your plans?"

If he was feigning confusion, he did it convincingly. "What the devil are you talking about?"

"I'm talking about Carazzan. He's gone."

Hugh stood up so quickly that the papers scattered across the floor. He ignored them. "Gone where?"

Seeds of doubt sprouted inside her. "I went to see him, to say goodbye, and his stall is empty."

"Perhaps one of the grooms is exercising him."

"And perhaps you couldn't wait to claim him."

"Adrienne, I swear..."

He moved toward her, and she shrank back. "Don't touch me. You've manipulated me all along, and I was stupid enough to fall for it." It was all becoming clear now. "I thought you hatched the idea of our engagement conveniently quickly, but I'll bet it was part of your plan all along. As my fiancé, you get the land, Carazzan and the benefit of my position in one tidy package."

She spun away, fighting tears. She would not cry in front of him. "You suspected that Cindy was in league with the media. You could have let her know where we were going, knowing she'd do exactly what she did, so you would be forced to defend my honor when it was what you wanted all along."

While she raged, he remained stonily silent. Then he said, "You missed your calling, princess. You should have been a fiction writer, coming up with a plot like that."

"I notice you don't deny it."

"Why should I? Where I come from, people are innocent until proven guilty, so the burden of proof is on you, Your Highness."

She cringed as he made her title sound like an insult. She had spoken out of hurt and anger. Could he possibly be innocent? Then she thought of the empty stall. "If you're telling the truth, where is Carazzan?"

"Cindy Cook?" he suggested.

"You don't think she would do such a thing?"

"You know what they say about hell's fury and a woman scorned?"

He sounded as if he meant Adrienne, she thought. He had scorned her but she hadn't betrayed him. Had he betrayed her?

As he picked up a phone, she asked, "What are you doing?"

"Getting your security people to investigate. A horse like Carazzan isn't easily hidden away. If Cindy took him, someone must have seen her."

It was what she should have done in the first place before coming in here with guns blazing, throwing out accusations that seemed crazy now, Adrienne thought. Her feelings for Hugh made it hard to think straight. She linked her hands, wanting to wring them instead, and willed herself to calmness.

When he finally hung up, she was in a fever of impatience. "What happens now?"

"We wait," he said shortly.

In spite of everything she longed to go to him and feel his strong arms enfolding her. Furious with herself, she held back. If Hugh was using her, she didn't want to make a bigger fool of herself than she had already done. It didn't stop her wanting him, needing him, loving him. The minutes ticked by like hours.

When the telephone rang, she jerked convulsively. Hugh picked it up. His end of the conversation told her nothing. "The culprit wasn't Cindy," he said tonelessly, in response to her questioning look as he hung up.

"Then who?"

"Not who, what. It seems one of the younger grooms was exercising Carazzan when the wild stallion with the white mane showed up. Looking for Gypsy would be my guess. Carazzan decided to see the intruder off his territory."

"Why didn't they tell me that Carazzan had run off?" Instead, she had made a complete idiot of herself by accusing Hugh.

"Evidently the kid went after Carazzan without telling anyone, hoping to get the horse to come back before you found out."

"And now?"

"Your people have located him in the foothills. He didn't have time to get far. He'll probably return on his own, now that he's seen off the intruder, so you'll have your horse back before nightfall."

The chill in Hugh's voice seeped into her soul. "He isn't my horse," she said in a voice barely above a whisper. "You won the challenge. He belongs to you now."

"So you've changed your mind about it being a conspiracy on my part?"

"Can you forgive me for saying such a thing?" If she hadn't been so desolate at the thought of losing Hugh, she never would have spoken so rashly.

He could forgive her just about anything, he thought. It still hurt that she hadn't trusted him, that she had suspected him of using her to get what he wanted. But one look at her bone-white face and trembling hands banished his anger, although the hurt remained. "There's nothing to forgive. You acted out of love, and I can't blame you for it. I'd probably have done the same."

But not the same love, she thought. The gulf between them widened into an unbridgeable chasm. "Then it's over," she said flatly.

He nodded. "I won't say it's been fun." More like slow torture, actually, spending day after day acting out an engagement that could never be real, no matter how much he wanted it. And he did. No point thinking of how much.

She moved restlessly, picking up objects from the desk and setting them down again for no reason he could see. "What will you do now?"

"What I came to Carramer to do. Establish the ranch and the breeding program. Your brother and I sorted out the final details today."

"And you'll take Carazzan with you?"

"No."

The flat negative brought her head up. "Why not?"

"Because he belongs to you and always did."

"But you won the challenge."

"That's moot, since you were a length in front of me before you did your Camille act."

She didn't smile. Her emotions felt too raw for that. "All the same, I didn't finish and you did." She hadn't forgotten seeing the jade marker on the ranger's desk.

"Not according to the records," he said softly.

She knew she looked as confused as she felt. "But the ranger credited you with the win, didn't he?" She knew the marker wasn't a product of her imagination.

"No, I told the ranger to log it in your name. You got to the marker a hair's breadth before I did."

"So you let me get the credit for the ride?" She could hardly believe he had done it, far less allow herself to consider what it might mean.

His handsome features twisted into a cynical smile. "Is it so hard to accept? I know you don't think much of me, but a leopard *can* change its spots. Big Dan Jordan taught me that much."

"I don't hold your background against you, Hugh."

He didn't need to say she had been quick enough to accuse him of taking Carazzan and being in league with Cindy against her. She saw it in his eyes. He had said there was nothing to forgive, but she suspected her mistrust would fester alongside all the other hurts he'd endured in his lifetime because of who he was.

She wished there was some way to erase the words, the hurt. But some things were beyond even a princess. She held herself stiffly as he came closer, but he stopped an arm's length away and made no move to touch her. "I won't come back, Your Highness," he said, the formality in his tone making her want to weep.

"What shall I tell the people about our engagement?"

"You can say...say that it was a mistake. Everyone's entitled to one."

But it wasn't a mistake, she wanted to cry out. It was the most rational move she had made in a long time.

His intense gaze jolted through her. "Will you be okay?"

She resisted the urge to laugh hysterically. She was a princess. They were always okay, even when they weren't. "I'll be fine," she responded.

"Good." He scooped up the papers from the floor and bundled them haphazardly into his attaché case. "Then I'll be on my way."

As the door closed behind him, she told herself she was glad he hadn't tried to kiss her goodbye. She might have broken into a thousand pieces if he had. It was better this way. A clean break. At least he had left her Carazzan.

He had left her Carazzan.

The thought rocketed through her like a shooting star on a clear night, lighting up the dark spaces in her mind so she could think clearly for the first time in a long while. He had left her the horse that he had acknowledged was the key to his dream of breeding the world's finest riding horse.

Without Carazzan, what would happen to his plans for the new ranch? Unless he planned to give that up, too. A chill gripped her as Michel's words came back to her. *She showed me with her actions.* Hugh's actions could mean only one thing, and she trembled as she allowed herself to think the unthinkable. Did he care about her more than he cared about his dream?

She had to know the truth.

Hampered by her healing injury, she wasn't fast enough to catch him before he had his driver take him to the helipad. Urgency gripped her as she considered her options. She could wait for the car to return, call for another, or go after Hugh by the fastest means at hand.

The stud manager didn't like the idea of her riding Gypsy, especially after the visit from the wild stallion. "Knowing Carazzan, the interloper won't dare come back again," she said.

The manager gave up and saddled the mare for her. She was streaking away toward the helipad before the man could ready another horse and accompany her. As Gypsy bolted along, Adrienne's thoughts flew as fast as the horse's hooves. What if she was too late? What if Hugh's helicopter left before she could reach him? What if she had misread his gesture?

She hadn't, she told herself. She was well aware of what it would have cost *her* to give up Carazzan, and that would have been to Hugh, the only man on earth she would have deferred to. This time she didn't think her trust was misplaced.

The helicopter blades churned air and dust as she approached. She called out, but Hugh didn't hear her above the spinning rotors. But he did see her. She saw him speak to the pilot, who opened the door. Hugh jumped to the ground.

He bent low until he was clear of the rotors, then straightened, fury blazing in his expression. "What the devil do you think you're doing, riding with that ankle barely healed?" he demanded.

She let his fury roll off her, but welcomed his help to dismount. "I was looking for you."

"Well you've found me. I only hope you haven't done yourself some damage."

Only to her heart, she thought, as exhilaration leaped through her. The feel of Hugh's hands spanning her waist set off a chain reaction of needs and wants that it was all she could do not to throw her arms around his neck and drag him against her.

Too many witnesses.

"I want you to come for a ride with me," she said.

He looked at her as if she'd lost her mind. Maybe she had. "Here? Now? I'm hardly dressed for riding, and the chopper's waiting."

She waved a hand imperiously. "Let them wait. Privilege of rank."

"Yours maybe, not mine."

"Mine will serve." She limped over to Hugh's driver, who watched the scene in bemused fascination. He listened then went to carry her message to the helicopter pilot.

Dusting off her hands, she returned to Hugh. "Now we can go for that ride."

He had the good sense not to argue further but swung himself into the saddle and reached for her hand, hoisting her up in front of him. "Where to?"

Her outstretched arm encompassed the green-clad hills surrounding the villa. "Up there, anywhere."

"You're crazy, Your Highness."

But he did as bidden, wheeling Gypsy around and aiming her at the forest-studded slopes. In the shelter of the trees, he pulled the mare up. "Is this far enough or shall I keep going?"

"This will do nicely, thank you."

He helped her to dismount, his hands lingering around her waist for longer than was strictly needed, she noticed with a thrill of pleasure. He looked as if releasing her was an effort.

She certainly hoped so. She faced him with hands on hips. "Now tell me why you decided to leave me Carazzan?"

"Why shouldn't I?"

"That horse is the key to your breeding plans."

"There are other horses."

"Not another like Carazzan."

"And not another like you," he said as if he couldn't keep the words back any longer.

"So the horse was a gift to a princess?"

"A gift to you," he amended.

"Because you care for me?"

The answer seemed to be wrung from him. "Yes."

"Yet you were about to get into that helicopter and fly away from me without a backward glance."

"Not quite," he assured her. "But I was doing what I had to do."

"So noble," she teased. "Did it occur to you that I might have something to say about it?"

"You can't." His voice was harsh, grating, as if he was going over old ground he'd covered in his mind many times.

Because she was too like his ex-wife, she read between the lines. It was time to prove otherwise. "You have two choices, Hugh. You can stay or you can leave. Either way you'll have to deal with me. If you leave, I'll give up my title, my right of succession, even my country if I must, but I shall follow you all the way back to America."

He stared at her, speechless at last. "You would do it for me?"

"If that's what it takes for us to be together."

She meant it, he saw from the fire in her eyes and the

determined lift of her chin. It was so exactly the opposite of what his ex-wife had done that any remaining comparison fled from his mind. He was forced to deal with Adrienne on her own terms, and the prospect drove the breath from his body.

"I can't," he said, his voice raw. "I won't let you give up so much on my account."

She felt her legs turn to water. She had been so sure he shared her feelings, so sure they could work this out. Doubt assailed her along with a soul-wrenching suspicion. "Because of the way I disappointed you before?"

He stared at her, genuinely baffled. "What are you talking about?"

"During our Wedding Eve at the cabin, you started to make love to me but stopped because my lack of experience disappointed you."

His breath rushed out. "Good Lord, Adrienne, it was precisely because I *wasn't* disappointed that I walked out. If I'd stayed, you wouldn't have lacked experience for much longer, and I'm fairly sure that your people frown on their princess being seduced before marriage."

Joy swelled through her at his words, driving out all doubt. He *had* wanted her, after all. Only consideration for her had made him walk away. "They're not as old-fashioned as all that," she said a little primly.

"But I am. If we make love, I wanted it to be on our wedding night."

Her heart did a quick double beat, and she pressed a hand to her throat. "What are you saying?"

He took her hands and lifted them to his mouth, grazing the knuckles with his lips as he looked deeply into her eyes. "I'm saying I love you, Adrienne."

She froze, hardly able to absorb the words she had waited so long to hear. "What did you say, Hugh?"

"I said I love you, princess. I've known it since I awoke beside you in the cabin, but I didn't think anything could possibly come of it. Until now. No one ever offered to give up a kingdom for me before."

"I'll do it gladly, if it means we can be together."

His wondering gaze fastened on her as if he could never get enough of the sight. "I think you mean it."

"I do." She gestured around them. "No title, no country, is going to keep me from you. I started falling in love with you from the moment you rescued me at the fair."

He shuddered, sharing the memory. "Little did I know who I was rescuing."

"What would you have done if you had known?"

He brushed a few strands of hair off her face with such casual intimacy that her breath caught. "I would still have taken care of you. It's become a habit I don't seem to be able to shake. But I would have tried to keep my emotions out of it, although it probably wouldn't have worked."

"It didn't for me," she confessed. "When I awoke in the ranger's office and saw you there, my knight in muddy armor, moving heaven and earth to get help for me, I knew beyond doubt that I loved you. Then to protect my reputation you told Lorne we were engaged, and I found I wanted it to be real more than I'd ever wanted anything before."

His heart almost burst. "I never meant to leave, you know. I couldn't."

"But you were about to take off."

He nodded. "It's true, the chopper was taking me to the airport for a flight back to America."

At her indrawn breath, he cupped the side of her face in a gentle hand. "Not for good. I intended to settle my affairs there and come back. Prince Michel will confirm it. At our meeting this morning I asked him about becoming a Car-ramer citizen."

The touch of his hand against her face made her long for more of his caresses. She turned her head slightly to kiss his palm, and a low moan ripped from his throat. He brought his other hand up to frame her face and fastened his mouth against hers.

She drank him in greedily, terrified at how close she had come to losing him. Not losing him, she reminded herself. He had planned to return for good. She was almost afraid to let herself think of what it meant. "What did Michel say about your request for citizenship?" she asked, her lips moving against his mouth.

He nibbled on her upper lip, and shards of sensation pierced her. "He said marriage would take care of it automatically."

He still hadn't asked her, she thought, fighting the fear that he wouldn't, even now. "Are you planning on getting married?"

"If the woman I love agrees." He took a breath to the limit of his lungs. "Adrienne, will you marry me?"

He felt the stillness grip her. Had she doubted it was what he wanted? He had said he loved her. What more—no, a woman needs to hear the words, he told himself. "I love you, Adrienne. I want you to be my wife, the mother of my children, the light of my life for all time."

She couldn't keep her eyes from brimming. But they were tears of pure happiness. Before they spilled and ruined her speech, she said, "Yes, I'll marry you, Hugh. I love you more than life itself."

He kissed her again, slowly, deeply, then drew away, sensing that her reluctance to part, even for a second, more than matched his own. "There's so much I want to share with you, the ranch, my dreams—"

She touched a finger to his lips. "I'll gladly share your dreams, Hugh, but that's not why I said yes. Your love is more than enough for me."

"And for me, princess."

She felt a smile bloom. "You won't be able to tease me about my title once you become my prince."

He let out a whistling breath. "That's quite a step for a boy from nowhere. I still have to adjust to being around while you do your royal thing. Is a title really necessary?"

"Your choice, but there's one title you can't refuse—my prince of hearts."

He let a slow grin develop. "Now, that I like." Taking her in his arms, he proceeded to show her how much, while she surrendered eagerly to the sovereignty of his love.

Epilogue

His wife had never looked more beautiful, Hugh thought as she carried their baby son into the church. The baby's title was bigger than he was, and a lump came to Hugh's throat as he imagined His Highness Daniel Lorne Michel de Marigny one day ruling over some part of Carramer.

His son, the prince.

It must be love making him so fanciful, because he had a sudden vision of a wide-eyed little boy watching the procession from the shelter of an alcove. The boy's figure was shadowy now, but Hugh fancied he wore torn pants, a shirt two sizes too big for his skinny frame, and no shoes. Himself at fourteen. Behind him, another shadowy figure, Big Dan Jordan, placed a beefy hand on the boy's shoulder.

"I did right by you both," Hugh told the image in his mind. Just as Adrienne had done right by him. Since their marriage eighteen months ago, she had made him happier than any man alive, just by existing in his world.

Her beauty, passion and love of life so exactly matched his own that she could have been made for him. His job as he saw it was to love her as she deserved to be loved. He had accepted a title only because it pleased her, not because he needed it. He had long ago made peace with who and what he was. But he could handle being Duke of Nuee if it made Adrienne happy. And dealing with royal life hadn't been as difficult as he'd thought. It had a lot in common with running any other business.

"How are you enjoying fatherhood?"

It was Prince Lorne, ruler of Carramer. Hugh was glad he'd managed to lose his initial awkwardness around the monarch. Now he liked and respected his brother-in-law, who had a tough job and did it with real style. "I could do with a bit more sleep, but Daniel's worth it," Hugh told him.

He saw Lorne's gaze go to his radiant wife, Princess Alison, and their son, Nori, who was holding the hand of his little sister, Aimee. "Children are always worth it. They're our future, after all."

"I think Caroline and Michel agree with you."

Lorne followed Hugh's gaze to where Michel's American bride was holding their eleven-month-old daughter, Rose. "Indeed they would. I have never seen Michel look happier or more settled."

Hugh felt a wide grin spill across his face. "I know exactly how he feels."

"Are we here for a christening or a mutual admiration society?" came a crusty voice behind them. Hugh recognized the doctor's voice at once. No one else dared to address Lorne so familiarly, but Hugh had grown accustomed to Alain Pascale's brusque manner. As physician to the royal family for longer than any of them could remember, he had presided over all the de Marigny births and had certain privileges.

He hadn't presided over Daniel's birth simply because

Daniel had chosen to start arriving early, at the foot of Mount Mayat where his parents had gone to celebrate the first anniversary of the challenge that had led to this moment.

Luckily, all had gone well because, for once, Adrienne had accepted Hugh's insistence that they take a retinue along. He had told her he had no intention of delivering his son himself on the side of a mountain, not realizing how close it would come to that.

As it was, Adrienne had been airlifted to hospital barely in time for Daniel's arrival. Dr. Pascale had been in Australia visiting his wife's family and still hadn't forgiven the couple for spoiling what he called his "perfect record."

"Baby turned out all right in spite of everything," Alain grumbled, but the fond look he gave Daniel belied his gruff words.

"I'll make sure you're around to deliver our next one," Hugh promised him.

"That's what you said this time." He glared at Hugh. "You give that little lady time to get over this one before you start planning the next."

"Yes, Doctor."

Alain looked as if Hugh's meek tone hadn't fooled him for a second, but he nodded acceptance. "At least you showed some sense in choosing the boy's godfathers," he said.

Lorne laughed. "Only because you're one of them."

"As I said, he showed good sense."

They were still laughing until silenced by a stern look from Adrienne. The christening was about to start. It gave Hugh another rush. Imagine his son being christened in a cathedral by the country's highest-ranking religious official.

But he got an even greater rush when Adrienne looked up at him. Her eyes were huge and moist, and twin roses of color bloomed high on her cheeks. With their baby son cradled against her breast she looked breathtaking. He wished the ceremony was over so he could have her to himself again.

First they had to go through the official ceremony, then there would be a formal reception. Only then could he be alone with his family. He glanced at Lorne and Michel. They did their duty with such dedication that Hugh wondered if he was the only one who had to fight resentment at how much time was taken away from his loved ones.

Prince Michel moved closer and gave Hugh a brotherly nudge. "How soon do you think this will be over? I ordered an electric train set as a christening gift for Daniel, and I can't wait to show it to him."

Hugh suppressed a grin. He wasn't alone after all. And he would never be alone again. They might be a royal family, but the most important word was *family*. After all the lonely years he finally belonged to someone and they to him. Gratitude wrapped itself around his heart like a cloak. He lifted his gaze to a magnificent stained-glass window above the altar and sent his heartfelt thanks winging upward before turning again to the woman he loved.

* * * * *

THE CARRAMER CROWN

If you missed any of the royal romances in Valerie Parv's *The Carramer Crown* series, here's a chance to order your copy today!

SR #1459   THE MONARCH'S SON $3.50 U.S.☐ $3.99 CAN.☐
SR #1465   THE PRINCE'S BRIDE-TO-BE $3.50 U.S.☐ $3.99 CAN.☐

(limited quantities available)

TOTAL AMOUNT	$
POSTAGE & HANDLING	$
($1.00 for one book, 50¢ for each additional)	
APPLICABLE TAXES*	$ _____
<u>**TOTAL PAYABLE**</u>	$ _____
(check or money order—please do not send cash)	

To order, send the completed form, along with a check or money order for the total above,
payable to **THE CARRAMER CROWN** to: In the U.S.: 3010 Walden Avenue, P.O. Box 9077,
Buffalo, NY 14269-9077; In Canada: P.O. Box 636, Fort Erie, Ontario L2A 5X3.

Name: _____

Address: _____ City: _____

State/Prov.: _____ Zip/Postal Code: _____

Account # (if applicable): _____   075 CSAS

  *New York residents remit applicable sales taxes.
  Canadian residents remit applicable GST and provincial taxes.

Where love comes alive™

Visit Silhouette at www.eHarlequin.com   SRTCC2

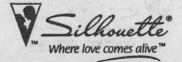

If you enjoyed what you just read,
then we've got an offer you can't resist!

Take 2 bestselling love stories FREE!

Plus get a FREE surprise gift!

where love comes alive—online...

Visit the *Author's Alcove*

- ➤ Find the most complete information anywhere on your favorite Silhouette author.
- ➤ Try your hand in the Writing Round Robin— contribute a chapter to an online book in the making.

Enter the *Reading Room*

- ➤ Experience an interactive novel—help determine the fate of a story being created now by one of your favorite authors.
- ➤ Join one of our reading groups and discuss your favorite book.

Drop into *Shop eHarlequin*

- ➤ Find the latest releases—read an excerpt or write a review for this month's Silhouette top sellers.
- ➤ Try out our amazing search feature—tell us your favorite theme, setting or time period and we'll find a book that's perfect for you.

All this and more available at

www.eHarlequin.com
on Women.com Networks

Silhouette
ROMANCE™

COMING NEXT MONTH

#1474 THE ACQUIRED BRIDE—Teresa Southwick
Storkville, USA
Single mother Dana Hewitt would do anything to keep her kids—even agree to a convenient marriage with tycoon Quentin McCormack! But then she began dreaming of being his real bride—in every sense of the word....

#1475 JESSIE'S EXPECTING—Kasey Michaels
The Chandlers Request...
Sweet Jessie Chandler had always loved Matthew Garvey from afar. But he had never noticed her—until an innocent kiss led to an unexpected night of passion. What would Matthew's reaction be once he learned Jessie's expecting?

#1476 SNOWBOUND SWEETHEART—Judy Christenberry
The Circle K Sisters
When city gal Lindsay Crawford became snowbound with handsome rancher Gil Daniels, she couldn't help falling for him. But he thought she wouldn't be happy with country living forever. Could she convince him that her home was where *he* was?

#1477 THE NANNY PROPOSAL—Donna Clayton
Single Doctor Dads
Greg Hamilton had his hands full raising his ten-month-old baby, and Jane Dale's motherly touch was just what the doctor ordered. Although Greg wasn't looking for a wife, seeing his pretty nanny rocking his baby triggered some unsettling feelings in his bachelor heart....

#1478 RAISING BABY JANE—Lilian Darcy
Allie Todd had vowed never to get close to another man again. Yet sharing close quarters with Connor Callahan while caring for her six-month-old niece had forged a bond between them that couldn't be denied—just like the secret she was keeping about the maternity of baby Jane....

#1479 ONE FIANCÉE TO GO, PLEASE—Jackie Braun
To secure the job of his dreams, Jack Maris asked Tess Donovan to pose as his fiancée. Savoring the distraction from her demanding life, Tess agreed. But when word of their engagement spread, they kept up the charade. And then things got deliciously complicated....

CMN0900